"This just

"If you're worried I'm going to fall in love with you again, don't." Her flushed cheeks turned a deeper shade of crimson, and somehow, she looked lovelier than ever. "Because I promise you I'm not."

"You sure about that, Elly Bean?"

No sooner had the words left his mouth than the truth hit him square in the chest. He wasn't worried about Ella falling for him. Quite the opposite.

They weren't kids anymore, and Ella Grace had grown into a beautiful woman with a beautiful soul. She was throwing him a lifeline, and all he could think about at the moment was her heart-shaped face and the tender way she'd interacted with Bethany.

"I've never been more sure of anything in my life."

Well, that settles that. A wave of something that felt too much like disappointment washed over him.

But Ella was still off-limits, right along with every other female on the planet. All Luke wanted was to build a healthy, stable home for Bethany. She was his first and only priority.

New York Times bestselling author **Teri Wilson** writes heartwarming, hope-filled, inspirational romance. Four of Teri's books have been adapted into Hallmark Channel movies, including fan favorite *Unleashing Mr. Darcy*. Teri is a recipient of the prestigious RITA® Award for excellence in romantic fiction and a recent inductee into the San Antonio Women's Hall of Fame. When not writing, Teri enjoys spreading doggy joy with her Cavalier King Charles spaniel, Charm, a registered therapy dog.

Books by Teri Wilson

Love Inspired

Alaskan Hearts
Alaskan Hero
Sleigh Bell Sweethearts
Alaskan Homecoming
Alaskan Sanctuary
Training Her Alaskan K-9

Special Edition

The Fortunes of Texas: Secrets of Fortune's Gold Ranch

A Fortune's Secret

Montana Mavericks: Six Brides for Six Brothers

The Maverick's Secret Baby

The Fortunes of Texas: Digging for Secrets

Fortune's Lone Star Twins

Visit the Author Profile page at LoveInspired.com for more titles.

TRAINING HER ALASKAN K-9

TERI WILSON

LOVE INSPIRED
INSPIRATIONAL ROMANCE

ISBN-13: 978-1-335-62140-5

Training Her Alaskan K-9

Love Inspired
22 Adelaide St. West, 41st Floor
Toronto, Ontario M5H 4E3, Canada
www.LoveInspired.com

HarperCollins Publishers
Macken House, 39/40 Mayor Street Upper,
Dublin 1, D01 C9W8, Ireland
www.HarperCollins.com

Printed in Lithuania

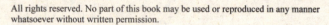

Casting all your care upon him; for he careth for you.
—*1 Peter* 5:7

For those who dream of Alaska—of wide-open skies painted with the Northern Lights, the tender hush of snowfall and snow-draped mountains that whisper adventure.

Chapter One

Ella Grace stumbled to a halt in the doorway of her office as she caught sight of a Labrador retriever who seemed to be making himself right at home. As the codirector of Helping Hounds Assistance Dogs, Ella interacted with dozens of dogs a day. Sometimes more. So the sight of the chocolate Lab wasn't altogether unexpected, except for the fact that he was currently standing smack on the center of her desk.

"Snickers, what on earth are you doing up there?"

The Lab wagged his tail and did a little tap dance on the neatly organized stack of behavioral assessments she'd been working on all morning. The pages didn't look quite so orderly anymore. One of them even appeared to have a bite taken out of the upper left-hand corner.

Ella narrowed her gaze at Snickers. "Aren't you supposed to be training for obstacles right now?"

The dog panted, pink tongue lolling out of the side of his mouth. Clearly he was more excited about making a mess of her office than he was about learning how to alert a human partner to unseen obstacles in their path. Not exactly stellar guide-dog behavior.

But at thirteen months old, Snickers was still young. Impulsivity aside, he had a lot of promise. Ella wasn't giving up on him yet. She just really needed to get all four of his paws back on the ground.

"Sit," she said in a firm but kind voice.

Snickers obeyed at once. Clearly pleased with himself, he wagged his tail even harder, sending what was left of Ella's neat stack of work flying off the desk. Puppy behavioral assessment reports rained down like confetti.

"Ella, are you in here? Oh, good. Someone dropped by——" Molly York, the Helping Hounds front desk attendant, went wide-eyed in the doorway and her voice drifted off as she took in the sight of Snickers. Someone stood behind her, just over her right shoulder.

Super. Just what Ella needed at the moment—an audience.

"Oh, wow," Molly said. "I guess Snickers is playing hooky again. How did he get up there?"

"Your guess is as good as mine. This little guy seems to have springs in his feet." Ella's gaze flitted to the dog, still sitting politely in response to her command. That had to count for something, didn't it?

She shifted her attention back toward Molly and the visitor, still mostly obscured by the receptionist. Although by the deep, amused cough that escaped him, she could tell it was a man.

She squared her shoulders and did her best to project a professional, capable, girl boss image—albeit one who currently had papers scattered all over the floor and a fifty-plus-pound puppy sitting atop her workspace. "What can I help you with?"

"Sorry, I got distracted there for a second. This gentleman stopped by for information on hearing dogs, and since you didn't have anything on the calendar right now, I thought you might want to speak with him." Molly stepped aside to make room for the visitor to enter the office. "This is…"

"Luke Tanner?" Ella blinked. Was she seeing things? What was he doing here?

He tilted his head, eyes crinkling in the corners the same way they'd always done back when he'd been the bad-boy hockey star of Snowhaven High. She'd been such a fool for that handsome face of his back then. Such a stupid, stupid fool. "Ella Grace?"

Molly glanced back and forth between them. "Oh, so you two already know each other?"

Luke nodded. "We do."

"We did," Ella said at the exact same time.

A wounded expression splashed across Luke's face, followed by a loaded silence. Then he rearranged his features into one of his trademark toothpaste-commercial-worthy smiles. Ever the charmer. "It was a while ago."

Truth.

And yet, in so many ways, it felt like yesterday. Unfortunately for Ella, most of those ways involved a fair amount of embarrassment, regret, and good old-fashioned heartbreak.

That's not altogether fair, a voice whispered from deep inside her.

Ella ignored it. She could deal with her conscience later, after she found out precisely why her older brother's best friend and—perhaps, more importantly—the object of her years-long schoolgirl crush, had just turned up at her office out of the blue. Luke had left Snowhaven, Alaska, in his rearview mirror before he'd given the ink on his high school diploma time to dry. He'd never given their hometown, or Ella, a backward glance. Even her brother Travis had lost touch with him in the decade that followed, and the two boys had been as thick as thieves when they'd been kids. But from what Ella heard via the Snowhaven grapevine, Luke had spent the past ten years traveling all over the Lower 48 as a journeyman hockey player in the minor leagues. His life didn't seem to lend itself to maintaining anything permanent, including relationships.

"We're good here, Molly. Thanks for showing Mr. Tanner to my office," Ella said.

"Sure thing. Would you like me to take Snickers back to class?"

Ella shook her head. "That's okay. I'll get him settled myself."

The last time she'd been alone with Luke, she'd humiliated herself beyond all belief. For this impromptu meeting she needed backup, even if that backup had four legs, a tail, and a bit of a naughty streak.

With a nod, Molly left the office and somehow seemed to take half the oxygen with her. Ella felt like a high school freshman all over again, wearing her cinnamon-colored hair in a high ponytail and her heart on her sleeve.

"*Mr.* Tanner? Seriously, Ella?" The corners of Luke's mouth quirked up, but the smile didn't quite reach his eyes. "I know it's been a while, but you used to cook tiny cakes in your Easy-Bake Oven for me and Travis every evening after hockey practice. Surely you can still call me Luke. Please?"

Of course, he'd referenced a memory that would remind her of the four-year age difference between them. It rankled. Didn't he realize they weren't kids anymore?

Heavenly Father, please help me get through this conversation. Ella swallowed. Once upon a time, she'd talked to God about Luke Tanner on a daily basis. Maybe things hadn't changed so much after all.

"Of course." She smiled, even as her stomach filled with a rebellious swarm of butterflies. "It's good to see you again…Luke."

"You, too." He glanced around the office and his attention paused on the shelf that held her collection of small, wooden animal carvings—handmade gifts her father had whittled when she was a little girl. Then his gaze lingered on Snickers. The dog dropped into a down position, rested his chin on his paws, and sighed. Apparently, he'd decided Ella's desk was comfy enough to stay a while. "So you work here, huh?"

"I'm the codirector, actually." *That's right. I'm a fully grown adult now.* "My friend Willow Bell and I started the business three years ago. Willow handles PR and fundraising, and I'm in charge of dog training and matching up our canines with the right clients."

She wasn't sure why she was explaining all of this to him, other than the fact that she tended to babble when she was nervous. A simple *yes* would've sufficed.

"I didn't expect to see you here, but the more I think about it, it makes perfect sense. You always did love animals." The tone of Luke's voice went tender. "And helping people."

It was a nice thing to say—nice enough that Ella was almost tempted to let down her guard. Emphasis on *almost*. At least he remembered something besides her Easy-Bake Oven and the ill-fated love letters she'd slipped into his locker during his senior year, when she'd been just a lowly freshman.

Hopefully, he'd forgotten the latter altogether. Would it be wrong to pray that he'd been struck by a very specific form of retrograde amnesia sometime during the past ten years?

Ella's attention snagged on the framed Bible verse from the Book of Isaiah that hung in a place of prominence on her office wall. *And I will bring the blind by a way that they knew not; I will lead them in paths that they have not known: I will make darkness light before them, and crooked things straight.* The verse served as the mission statement for Helping Hounds, and on challenging days, it also reminded Ella that she wasn't the one in charge around here. God was.

Right. So if Luke Tanner had turned up in her office out of the blue, there had to be a good reason for it, regardless of her personal feelings about the man.

"Have a seat." She gestured to one of the chairs situated opposite her desk. "What can I help you with? Molly said you dropped by for information about our hearing-dog program?"

Ella crossed her arms and leaned against the edge of her desk directly across from Luke, since occupying her chair would've forced her to peer around a giant lump of chocolate Lab to meet his gaze. Snickers hadn't budged so much as an inch.

"I did." Luke's attention strayed toward the dog. "Can I pet this one, or is he working?"

"I see you've done a bit of homework on assistance dogs." Ella grinned. More often than not, members of the general public didn't realize they weren't supposed to interact with an on-duty guide dog. "And, yes, you can pet him. Snickers is on a break right now."

Luke offered his hand for a sniff before scratching Snickers behind his ears. He smiled up at Ella as the Lab leaned into his touch. "He's sweet, but does he always take his break on your desk?"

"No, this is a first. Snickers is one of our guide dogs in

training. Most of the dogs at Helping Hounds are trained to assist people experiencing blindness or low vision. We just started our hearing-dog program earlier this year." Ella reached for a brochure and handed it to Luke. "Hearing dogs are trained to support the needs of people with hearing impairment and deafness. They can alert their owners to common household sounds and help them navigate the outside world with an increased sense of security."

"That's exactly why I'm interested in one." He stared intently at the brochure for a beat before turning serious eyes on Ella. "The part about an increased sense of security."

Ella swallowed. His mood had shifted enough that she knew this wasn't simply a casual fact-finding mission. Luke needed help. "Is one of your friends or family members dealing with hearing loss?"

She assumed it must be his grandmother. Luke's parents had moved to the Lower 48 years ago, and Ella couldn't imagine who else he might still know here in Snowhaven.

"Yes." He took a deep breath, and the creases in the corners of his eyes didn't look so much like laugh lines anymore. "It's my little girl."

Ella's breath caught in her throat. *Luke has a child.* The news shouldn't have come as such a shock, but somehow it did. Her gaze darted to his bare ring finger before she could stop it.

He noticed, because, of course, he did.

The knowing look he gave her was sympathetic enough to tell her that he remembered the love letters after all. Every mortifying word of them.

Great. Now, he apparently thought she was still carrying a torch for him all these years later. Which she most definitely was *not*. She was just curious, that's all. The only times she'd imagined Luke standing in a tuxedo and waiting at the end of a church aisle, the bride walking toward him in a fluffy white gown had been her.

No ring. She wondered what that meant.

Pathetic much? Her cheeks flared with heat, and Snickers let out a curious whine. *Not now, Snickers. Please.*

"She's actually my niece," Luke said. "My brother passed away three months ago, and I'm now her legal guardian. The adoption paperwork should go through sometime soon."

A lump sprang immediately to Ella's throat. "Oh, Luke. I'm so sorry to hear about Steven."

Luke's younger brother had graduated just two short years before Ella. He'd been the class valedictorian and earned a full-ride scholarship to Oregon State. The two brothers were like opposite sides of the same coin, but both larger than life.

"Thank you. I'm—*we're*—adjusting. It's been a bit of a struggle, and I have such fond memories of growing up here that I thought moving back might be the best thing for Bethany." Luke raked a hand through his hair, a move Ella had seen him make a thousand times after removing his hockey helmet.

This whole encounter was disorienting. She felt like she had one foot in the past and the other in a dizzying, unfathomable present. Finding a dog on her desk suddenly seemed like the least surprising part of her day.

"Bethany is your niece?" she asked.

Luke nodded. "She's been deaf since birth, and her mother is no longer in the picture. It's just Bethany and me now."

"How old is she?"

"She's eight. Just started third grade last fall. Since school is on winter break, it seemed like the right time to make a change." He shook his head, dropping his gaze to his folded hands. "She's having a hard time, Elly Bean. I recently heard about hearing dogs, and I'll be honest. Something like that sounds like it could be a blessing."

Elly Bean. No one had called her that in years. She crossed her arms over her chest before her heart did something dumb, like skip a beat.

She took a deep breath, bracing herself to give him the bad news. "I'd love to help you. I really would…"

A muscle ticked in Luke's chiseled jaw. "But?"

"But…" Ella inhaled a steadying breath and reminded herself she wasn't doing anything wrong. She had to tell people *no* all the time. Luke wasn't different than any other potential client.

This *felt* different, though.

Which was precisely why the fact that she couldn't do anything for Luke and Bethany was for the best.

"I'm afraid that guides and hearing dogs typically aren't paired with handlers under the age of eighteen. Fifteen or sixteen, at the youngest. Working with a guide or hearing dog takes a certain level of maturity and commitment. Due to the intense training regimen needed for a dog to become a hearing guide, the handler is expected to spend nearly every waking hour with the canine." Ella studiously avoided looking at Snickers, who wasn't helping matters, given his off-the-charts cuteness factor. "Eight is awfully young for that kind of responsibility."

Luke blew out a long, tense breath. His blue eyes blazed bluer than ever. "But what if it's an extenuating circumstance?"

He wasn't making this easy. The entire reason Ella had gone into her line of work was to help people. That, plus her love of dogs. She hated having to turn anyone down.

He's not just anyone.

Her throat was as dry as sandpaper. "Even if I could somehow make an exception, I can't. We have a waiting list for both guide and hearing dogs. Pairing the right client with the right dog typically takes six months or more. Again, I'm sorry. I wish there was something I could do. The process takes time. It takes a lot of preparation to become a guide dog."

Luke's eyes cut toward Snickers.

"I can see that," he said flatly.

"Excuse me?" Ella blinked, wounded. "Snickers is a puppy. He's still training."

Luke held up his hands. "I'm sorry. I didn't mean to offend you. I'm just..."

Desperate.

He didn't need to say it out loud. The word was written all over his face.

Still, she hated the way one wrong word out of him could make her feel like a silly little girl all over again. She was good at what she did. She shouldn't have to feel like she needed to prove herself to anyone—least of all, the grown-up version of a boy who'd never seen her as anything more than his best friend's thoroughly forgettable younger sister.

She drew herself up to her full height and straightened the hem of her Helping Hounds hoodie. In this particular instance, it would've been nice if she'd been wearing something more polished than skinny jeans and her favorite polka-dot sneakers, but she worked with dogs all day. Funny how she never thought of her appearance as juvenile until now.

"I'm glad you stopped by. Feel free to keep the brochure, and maybe later down the line when Bethany is older, we can work something out." Ella pasted a smile on her face and muttered something about wishing she could do more to help.

She honestly wasn't sure what else she said. All she wanted was for him to leave so her heart would stop doing the awful thump-thump-thump thing in her chest, and she could go back to feeling like a fully competent professional woman who ran her own successful business and now cooked brownies in an actual, adult-size oven.

Still, her parting words to Luke lingered on the tip of her tongue, sweet like honey.

I wish I could do more to help.

Ella closed her eyes and pressed the heel of her hand against her breastbone until her galloping heartbeat returned to normal. When her eyelashes fluttered open again, the first thing her gaze landed on was the framed verse from Isaiah. And a still, small voice seemed to whisper in her ear.

Be careful what you wish for.

Ella Grace. Luke wiped down the food counter at the skating rink and stared out absently over the rutted white ice. *Elly Bean.*

He'd suspected he might run into Travis's younger sister eventually, but he hadn't been ready to bump into her on his very first day back in Snowhaven. A little warning would've been nice. Then again, who would've thought to warn him? Other than Gran, he hadn't spoken to anyone in his hometown for years.

This whole idea was beginning to feel like a mistake.

Luke gritted his teeth. *Too late.* The deed on the rink had been signed and notarized weeks ago, long-distance. The movers were unpacking all of his and Bethany's belongings at Gran's right this very second. Bethany was already trying on skates, teetering around the carpeted lobby on wobbly ankles.

Like most of Luke's choices over the past decade, the decision to come back to Alaska had been made on a whim. He'd been at the end of his rope. Life since Steven's fatal car accident three months ago had been little more than a blur. One minute, Luke had been on a rickety bus with the rest of his minor league hockey team, and the next, a lawyer had looked him in the eyes and told him he'd been appointed Bethany's guardian.

Their parents had given him an immediate out, volunteering to take in the child so he could continue crisscrossing the country, chasing a puck around a different patch of ice every few days. It shamed Luke to admit that he'd nearly agreed. Steven had chosen him, though. The thought of letting down his brother was inconceivable… almost as inconceivable as turning his back on a little girl who'd just lost her daddy after being abandoned by her mother when she was just a baby. Luke just couldn't do it.

"How's it going there, kiddo?" Luke asked, signing the words as he said them out loud. His ASL skills were seriously lacking, but he was working on it. Just like he was working on everything else. "Did you find a pair that fit?"

Bethany's little head bobbed up and down.

He wished she'd try speaking, the way she had before Steven's accident. Now, she barely even signed anymore.

At first, Luke had chalked up her silence to grief. It was a logical assumption. It wasn't until the school principal called two months after Luke had moved into his brother's house that he learned she was being bullied by a group of third-grade mean girls.

What kind of children made fun of a deaf girl's speaking voice mere months after her father passed away? Luke still couldn't wrap his head around it. He'd been at a complete and utter loss as to what to do. He was new at the parenting thing, in way, *way* over his head.

Despite his reputation as a troublemaker, Luke had always felt secure as a kid. Safe. Protected. Late one night, after the pull of nostalgia had him doing an online search for real estate in Snowhaven, he'd learned that the old skating rink where he and Steven had first learned how to play hockey was up for sale. It had felt like a sign, like a tiny glimmer of hope in the midst of so much darkness.

When he'd discovered that Snowhaven was now home to its own guide-and-hearing-dog training center, he'd been even more convinced that plunking down every last dime of his savings for the rink was the right decision. Since Gran had recently relocated to an assisted-living community, she'd insisted Luke and Bethany move into her vacated mountain cottage. Everything had fallen so nicely into place. For once in his life, Luke's wandering spirit was ready to settle down and do the right thing. And this *was* the right thing.

Or so he'd thought, especially after he'd dropped off Bethany with Gran this morning so he could visit Helping Hounds. Seeing Ella Grace there had felt like another sign. Steven's trust in him hadn't been misplaced, no matter what their parents thought.

But then Ella had roundly struck down the idea of getting Bethany a hearing dog, reminding Luke that coming back to Snowhaven wasn't the cure-all that he thought it was. Luke couldn't simply swoop into town and turn back the clock. If he could, he would've gone back to senior year and handled things differently the moment he'd found out that Ella had been the one leaving notes in his locker all year.

That's ancient history. You have more pressing problems now, remember?

Oh, how he wished he could forget.

He took in the shabby state of the rink. The smell of mildew hung in the air. Bethany looked like a newborn giraffe trying to balance on her skates.

"Let me help you get those laced up, sweetheart." Luke came around the counter, dropped to one knee, and went to work on her laces.

He should've bought her a brand-new pair of skates before they got to Alaska. He should've been nicer to Ella earlier today at Helping Hounds. He should've done a lot of things differently.

God, please still be there. I really need You right now. We both do.

Luke had never felt as close to God as he had when he lived in Snowhaven. Maybe that was another reason he'd come back. Or maybe he was just fooling himself, and it was too late to rediscover the faith of his youth.

"Uncle Luke," Bethany signed. The corners of her mouth pulled down into a frown.

"Yeah, kiddo? What's wrong? Are the skates too tight?"

"Are we going to stay in Alaska forever?" Her little fingers stretched out the sign for the word *forever*.

"We are." Luke nodded, despite his initial urge to hedge his bets and say "for a while" instead. He was a true journeyman player. Twelve teams in ten years. If pressed, he probably couldn't even name all the cities he'd called home in the past decade. "Your daddy and I grew up in Snowhaven. He learned to skate right here in this very building, and now, you will, too."

"But what about my mother?" Bethany signed.

Luke's hands stilled on the worn skate laces. His throat went dry. This was the first time Bethany had mentioned her mom since Steven died. The woman hadn't been part of the child's life since infancy.

"What about her, sweetheart?" he asked, speaking extra slowly so she could read his lips.

"What if she comes looking for me in Oregon and we're not there anymore?" Bethany's bottom lip slipped between her teeth.

"Um…" A rock settled in the pit of Luke's gut. Steven had never told Luke what, if anything, he'd said to Bethany about her mother. At the time, she'd been too young to understand the concept of divorce or a mother signing away her parental rights. Luke didn't know how to begin to explain it. Nor did he have it in him to tell her that her mother wasn't coming back for her. Not now, not ever. "Don't you worry. I made sure to leave our forwarding address. And Grandma and Grandpa are still in Eugene. They'll keep an eye on things back there for us. Everything is going to be okay. I promise."

He didn't have the heart to utter the crushing, unspoken truth.

I'm all you've got now, kiddo.

Chapter Two

Ella had absolutely no reason to feel bad about the way her impromptu meeting with Luke had gone. She'd simply been doing her job. That's what she told herself, anyway, as she got Snickers settled back in his training class and cleaned up the mess in her office.

Still, guilt tugged at her conscience for the rest of the day. By late afternoon, she was grateful to have an appointment out of the office that would surely require every last bit of her concentration so her thoughts would stop straying back to Luke and his little girl.

"Off to the shelter?" Molly looked up from her spot at the reception desk as Ella slid her arms into her down puffer coat and fished around in her pockets for her mittens.

"Yep. It's that time of the week," she said, tugging one of the mittens into place.

Once a week, Ella paid a visit to the animal shelter in Anchorage, situated just thirty miles north of Snowhaven. The shelter served the surrounding area, from the towns bordering the east side of the Cook Inlet, all the way down to Kenai. Back in high school, Ella had volunteered there, walking dogs on the weekends. A lot of the animals that turned up in the shelter, either as strays or owner surrenders, were Alaskan huskies, perfect for sledding. But Labs were very popular in Alaska, too. As were golden retrievers and German shepherds. Every year, she ended up rescuing a handful of dogs for the Helping Hounds training program. Most of Helping Hounds' puppies came from carefully selected breeders, but one of Ella's big goals was to use as many rescue dogs as possible as guides and hearing dogs. It was a win-win situation for everyone involved.

"Maybe you'll find a new recruit," Molly said.

"I hope so." Ella waved and pushed through the double doors.

Snow and salt crunched underfoot as she made her way to her SUV, and her breath hung in the air in little puffs of vapor. The shelter dogs were sure to be riled up by the recent snowfall, especially the huskies. They always loved it when winter set in.

Flurries danced against the windshield as Ella navigated the winding roads that hugged Cook Inlet on the way to the city. Tall, slender spruce trees lined either side, their branches tipping with snow. The shelter was located on the outskirts of town, with a view of the jagged Chugach Mountains on one side and the glassy black water of the inlet on the other. A carved wooden sign that read Frosty Paws Animal Rescue hung above the door.

"Hey there, Ella." Hunter Lockwood, the shelter manager, grinned as she entered the modest building. "Good to see you again."

Ella tugged off her mittens and stuffed them into her coat pockets. "Hey, Hunter. Nice to see you, too. Any good prospects this week?"

"Maybe." He shrugged one shoulder. "You're the expert, so you're going to have to see for yourself. A golden-doodle came in just last night. She hasn't been here long enough for me to get a good read on her, but she seems like a sweetheart. And I've got a shepherd mix and a yellow Lab you'll want to check out."

"That's amazing. Can't wait." Could she really manage to find three new rescues with guide-dog potential? Just thinking about it lifted her spirits. "Lead the way."

Evaluating rescue dogs to determine if they might be candidates for any type of guide or service-dog training was a complicated task. First and foremost was the animal's temperament. It was important for guide dogs to enjoy the company of humans and have an easygoing nature. With Hunter's help, Ella took each dog out to the meet-and-greet area to get an idea of its personality.

As expected, the goldendoodle was cheery and boisterous. She appeared to be just a year old, and Hunter said she'd come in as an owner surrender—unfortunately, a common scenario in animal rescue once dogs grew out of the cute little-puppy phase and became energetic adolescent dogs in need of proper training. But after the first few minutes in the meet-and-greet area, the dog calmed down a bit. Ella offered her a treat and she took it nicely. After a few cues, Ella was even able to teach the dog to sit.

"What a good girl. I think she'd be a great addition to our training program." Ella nodded at Hunter. They'd worked together long enough for Hunter to have a good idea of the qualities Ella looked for in a guide-dog candidate. He'd been spot-on about the goldendoodle.

She ruffled the curly gold hair on top of the dog's head. "What do you say, girl? Do you want to come with me and learn how to be a special helper for someone?"

The goldendoodle licked her hand.

One down, two to go.

The yellow Lab also possessed a nice temperament,

but when Ella threw a tennis ball for him to evaluate his movement, he favored his back right leg. She doubted he'd be up for the physically demanding task of being a guide. Plus, it made Ella second-guess his age. Because training took such a long time, she typically didn't take rescue dogs older than two and a half in order to extend the dog's working life for as long as possible.

The shepherd mix was a bit on the shy side. The poor thing tensed up when Ella tried to pet her, which could've simply been because the dog was nervous in a shelter environment. But touch sensitivity was a really important factor for a dog who would be required to wear a mobility harness or alert deaf handlers using physical cues. Ella had to go with her instincts and pass.

"Looks like it's just you and me," she said to the goldendoodle as Hunter removed the dog from her kennel and handed Ella her leash.

"Sorry the others didn't work out," Hunter said.

"No worries at all. I'm thrilled to have even one addition to the program." This was exactly what Ella had needed. For the first time since Luke had turned up at her office unannounced, she felt like herself again. The nagging sense of concern for him and his niece that had been clinging to her all day was finally gone.

She released a long exhale, and her shoulders relaxed. The ball of tension at the base of her neck loosened. Then she wrapped the goldendoodle's leash snugly around her hand and took one last glance around the kennel area.

Ella's gaze snagged on a small dog situated in one of the elevated cages on the back wall. Melting brown eyes peered at her from across the room. The dog's feathery tail wagged like mad.

"Is that what I think it is?" Ella pointed at the crate while the goldendoodle attempted to drag her out of the room.

Hunter glanced over his shoulder toward the small pup. "Sure is. A purebred Cavalier King Charles spaniel. Only six months old. We don't see very many of those here at the shelter. In fact, she might be the first."

"What a cutie." Ella drifted toward the puppy's kennel.

Hunter shook his head. "I hate to break it to you, but I doubt that one would make a great guide dog."

Guide dogs needed to be large enough to support a person's weight if they stumbled, fell down, or needed help. That definitely ruled out a Cavalier, who likely wouldn't tip the scales at twenty pounds, even fully grown.

"No, but I could see a tiny spaniel as a hearing dog," Ella countered. Hearing dogs just needed to be people-oriented, calm, and naturally attentive to sounds. She could almost tell simply by looking at the dog that it ticked off the first two qualities on the list.

She reached a hand toward the kennel, and the puppy licked her fingers through the bars, tail thumping against the floor of her crate.

"Not that one, I'm afraid." Hunter came to a stop beside her and sighed, attention fixed on the cheery little Cavalier. "She's deaf."

"Deaf? Seriously? She's so young." Ella's heart seemed to turn over in her chest.

"She was born with congenital deafness. The breeder thinks it might've been caused by an infection her mother had before the puppies were born," Hunter said.

Deaf since birth, just like Luke's niece.

So much for not thinking about Luke and Bethany.

It had to be a coincidence, didn't it? Except Ella didn't believe in coincidences. She believed in quiet moments of direction from God—what some people thought of as signs. She could remember a conversation with Luke years ago about this very thing. He'd pressed her, wanting to know how she could be certain that God was really telling her to do something. Ella had simply said she couldn't. That's what faith was all about—trusting in something unseen and unknowable.

Besides, what could it hurt to obey a perceived good impulse, even if she might never know whether it was a genuine spiritual prompting?

In this case, it could hurt a lot. Ella bit down hard on her bottom lip. *A whole lot.*

Hunter reached to unlatch the kennel, scooped up the Cavalier with one hand, and placed her in Ella's arms. The dog was all softness and warmth as she cuddled sweetly into the curve of her elbow. Ella couldn't help but smile.

Definitely not a coincidence.

The puppy nuzzled into the crook of her neck.

"So she's a breeder surrender, then?" Ella asked. At least that meant Hunter would have some information about the dog's background and breeding.

"Yup. The rest of the litter sold right away, but he couldn't find anyone willing to pay for this one." Hunter gave the puppy a scratch under her chin. "Cavaliers are as sweet and gentle as they come. I didn't expect her to be here long, but it's been six days and we haven't had any bites. It's a shame, really. She's gotten a lot of interest, but when people find out she's deaf, they change their minds."

"A shame," Ella murmured, gazing into the dog's big round eyes.

"Wait a minute. I know that look on your face." Hunter gave her a lopsided grin. "Anyone who works in dog rescue knows that expression only means one thing. You want to adopt her, don't you?"

No...

Yes?

Maybe.

Was she really going to do this?

Ella's heart rose to her throat. She had no clue if this was going to work. She almost hoped it wouldn't. "I think I might have an idea."

"I'm not sure, Gran. I think coming here might have been a mistake." Luke lowered his voice the following morning as he visited his grandmother in her room at Snowhaven Assisted Living.

Luke was stretched out in one of two matching recliners facing the television, permanently set to the home renovation channel. Bethany sat on a small sofa in front of a TV tray topped with her new Alaskan-themed coloring book spread open to a picture of a smiling bear with a salmon hanging from his mouth. The coloring book had been a gift from Gran, as was the accompanying jumbo-size box of crayons. Luke could've saved his grandmother the expense of purchasing such a large selection of crayons since Bethany liked to color anything and everything pink—her self-proclaimed favorite hue. Sure enough, she plucked a crayon labeled "pink carnation" from the box and began filling in the bear's shaggy coat. Luke had to admire her determination to see the world through her own version of rose-colored glasses, even if it made her trust in people too easily—people like her mother and the girls who'd bullied her at school.

"A mistake?" Gran glanced up from the yarn and crochet hook in her hands. "Why would you say that? You only just got here yesterday."

Luke scrubbed a hand over his face. He'd hardly gotten any sleep the night before. Every time he closed his eyes, his mind spun with all the ways he'd just turned Bethany's life upside down. And for what?

He'd actually thought coming back to Alaska would change everything. He'd placed such faith in the nostalgia of his childhood that he'd expected Bethany to instantly feel at home here. To feel safe.

Loved.

"Let's just say things aren't panning out quite like I'd hoped." His gaze flitted to Bethany, earnestly coloring a jagged mountain with a cotton-candy-tinted crayon. "School starts up again soon, and I'm not sure we're ready."

He'd already received an email from Bethany's teacher, and just reading it had filled Luke with dread. She'd seemed perfectly nice, but so had the teacher back in Oregon. Besides, it wasn't the staff Luke worried about so much as the students. If he could send Bethany to school wrapped in metaphorical bubble wrap, he'd do it in a heartbeat.

"This is a whole new beginning for both of you, dear. I think Bethany might be more ready for it than you are," Gran said.

Luke exhaled, shoulders dropping. "Have I mentioned that the rink is a total disaster?"

"You'll get it fixed up. Don't worry. New starts don't happen overnight, you know. The process takes time," Gran said, hands moving rhythmically over her crocheting.

The process takes time.

Those were the same exact words Ella had used yester-day when she'd been talking about training service dogs. Maybe God was trying to tell him something.

Or maybe Luke was right, and he had no business rais-ing an eight-year-old girl.

His gut twisted. He'd given up everything to honor his brother's wishes. He couldn't screw this up. Being a par-ent wasn't like playing hockey. He couldn't just switch teams and move on when the going got tough. Intellec-tually, Luke knew this. But he was already getting that itch—the familiar tug to pack it in and walk away.

Shame spiraled through him. Why was he like this? Better yet, why had Steven chosen him? That was the question that kept Luke up at night. What had his younger brother seen in him that made him think Luke would be the right person to raise Bethany if anything ever hap-pened to him? Because something *had* happened, and now Luke was drowning. Even in his youth, he'd been the trou-blemaker in the family. Steven had been the golden boy, and Luke had been all too happy to lean into his role as a disappointment to their parents. It was easier than fight-ing it. Eventually, getting into trouble became the only way to get their dad's attention, whether it meant skip-ping school or taking the blame for a hockey puck crash-ing through the window when, in fact, that little incident had been Steven's doing. But even before all of that, Luke had never been prone to irrepressible optimism.

Not like Ella, for instance.

She'd always found the good in everything—even in him, when he'd been wholly undeserving of her school-girl adoration. If her fervent belief in the chocolate Lab that had splayed himself all over her desk yesterday was any indication, she hadn't changed a bit.

"I'll tell you exactly what you should do," Gran said, setting aside her yarn.

Luke leaned forward, eager to glean whatever wisdom he could from his grandmother. Other than Steven, she was the only person in the family who'd always been there for him. Once, when he was a teenager, he'd overheard a tense conversation between Gran and his father. As Dad's mother, she was the only one who got away with challenging the man...about *anything*. This particular discussion had been about Luke, though. She'd urged Dad to spend more time with him to try and figure out the reason he kept acting out.

Afterward, Luke hoped things would change, but they never had.

He tensed, bracing against the memory as he waited for Gran's advice. Before she could say another word, a knock sounded on her door.

"That's probably the dietitian coming round so I can choose my meals for the week. They run a tight ship around here," Gran explained. She swiveled to face the door. "Come on in."

Luke closed his eyes, fighting the pull of sleep. He must have been even more tired than he realized because when he opened his eyes and glanced at the woman standing in the doorway, he almost thought it was Ella.

Wait a minute. Luke's gaze narrowed. It *was* Ella.

"Hello, Mrs. Tanner. I'm so sorry to barge in like this, but—" Ella's attention shifted from Gran to Luke. A thousand emotions seemed to flit across her face all at once. "Oh, you're here."

Did she consider that good news or bad? He honestly couldn't tell.

Luke stood.

"Ella." In his periphery, he saw Bethany's pink crayon drop onto the TV tray as her eyes grew as big as saucers—a reaction he chalked up to the absurdly cute puppy in Ella's arms.

The little dog was black and white with tan markings on its cheeks, above its eyes, and on the underside of its silky black ears. But by far the most prominent feature was the pup's pair of soulful brown eyes. The creature was as cute as a button. Nearly as cute as Ella.

Luke bit back a smile. The woman was some sort of dog magnet, just like she'd been back in the day, when she'd saved every scrawny stray that crossed her path. But what was she doing here?

He wondered briefly if she brought puppies around to visit residents of the assisted-living facility. It seemed like the sort of thing Ella would be involved with. Gran appeared just as surprised to see her as he was, though.

"Ella Grace, I thought that was you!" Like everyone else in Snowhaven, Gran had always thought Ella hung the moon.

His grandmother struggled to pull herself out of her recliner, and the ball of yarn tumbled from her lap. It hit the ground with a soft thud and rolled across the floor. The puppy cocked its head and followed the movement with its big round eyes, prompting a giggle from Bethany.

Luke was so unfamiliar with the sound of Bethany's laughter that it forced a double take out of him.

"Please don't get up," Ella said, chasing after the yarn and handing it back to Gran. "Like I said, I feel awful about showing up unannounced like this. I was actually just stopping by to see if you could help me get in touch with Luke." She cleared her throat and her gaze flitted in his direction again. Was it Luke's imagination, or did her smile stiffen ever so slightly? "But here you are."

"Here I am," he said, as Gran gave the two of them a curious glance.

Then Ella looked away again and her expression morphed back into its usual unguarded, tenderhearted countenance as her attention fell on Bethany.

"Hi, there," she signed with one hand while maintaining her grasp on the little dog with the other. "I'm Ella."

Of course, she knew ASL, and Luke could already tell she was far more proficient at it than he was.

He moved to stand next to Bethany. "Ella, this is my niece. Bethany, Miss Ella is an old friend of mine."

His signing felt clumsy and stilted compared to Ella's. The fact that her appearance had caught him completely off guard wasn't helping matters, but Bethany didn't seem to notice. She only had eyes for the puppy.

"May I pet your dog, Miss Ella?" The little girl's hands moved so fast that Luke could barely keep up with what she said, but the sentiment was clear. Anticipation rolled off her in waves.

"How polite of you to ask permission like that." Ella aimed a smile at Luke, as if he could take credit for Bethany's good manners. He couldn't. That was all Steven's doing. "Of course, you can pet her. I think she'd like that very much. In fact, perhaps you and Gran could puppysit her for just a second while I talk to your Uncle Luke in private real quick?"

Bethany gasped and her head spun in Gran's direction.

Gran winked and nodded her permission. "That would be lovely. We'd be happy to watch that little sweetheart, wouldn't we, Bethany?"

Bethany beamed as Ella instructed her to sit cross-legged on the floor and placed the dog in her lap. The puppy was unexpectedly gentle, content to simply gaze up at the child and be petted, tail wagging furiously. When the dog gave Bethany's cheek a tender lick, the little girl grinned up at Luke and his heart felt like it was being squeezed in a vise.

He cleared his throat and regarded Ella. As nice as this was, he still couldn't figure out why she was here when she'd so succinctly shot down the idea of a hearing dog less than twenty-four hours before.

"Shall we?" He gestured toward the hallway, the only place he could conceivably think of to have a word alone with her.

She nodded, but her eyes were still wary every time she looked at him, which struck Luke as profoundly sad. She never used to look at him like that. He understood, though. He'd broken her tender heart, even though for once in his life, he'd actually been trying to do the right thing. Intentions hadn't mattered back then, and he was starting to wonder if they ever would...with Ella, with Bethany, with this whole new life.

Ella nodded. "Sure."

And then she stalked toward the hallway with the enthusiasm of a person walking the plank, leaving Luke with the distinct impression that she wasn't sure at all. Not about him, anyway.

Chapter Three

Ella's pulse kicked up a notch or three once she and Luke were alone together in the hallway. Ridiculous, really. They were in a retirement center with his grandmother and niece just on the other side of the door. It was hardly a recipe for romance. There was no reason whatsoever for her to feel like she'd just hopped off a treadmill, heart pounding and breathless.

This was why she didn't date. It was too confusing… too *unsettling*. It had taken years after the love-letter embarrassment for Ella to entertain the notion of a relationship. Even then, she'd only gone out with guys she considered friends. She much preferred feeling like she had some sort of control over her emotions to throwing caution to the wind and letting herself fall head over heels for someone again.

And that had always worked, until the boyfriend she'd had two years ago wanted more. After that spectacular disaster, she'd decided to take a break from dating altogether.

But why was the topic suddenly rearing its head again now that Luke was back?

"You okay, Elly Bean?" He looked at her askance. "You seem a little tense."

"I'm fine." *One-hundred-percent a-okay. Not attracted to you in the slightest bit.*

She should probably ask him to stop calling her Elly Bean. It was juvenile. Also, nicknames implied some sort of intimacy, and she had every intention of keeping Luke at arm's length. She was here for his niece, not him.

But she couldn't seem to force the words out of her mouth. Instead, she lifted her chin so she could look him square in the eyes, and then she got straight to the point. "I think I found the perfect dog for Bethany."

A line etched between Luke's eyebrows. "I thought you said she was too young for a hearing dog."

"She is." Ella nodded. "But after you left yesterday, I had an appointment at the animal shelter, and I stumbled upon the perfect match for her. How would you feel about an emotional-support dog instead of a service animal?"

"An emotional-support dog?" Luke echoed.

"Yes. Emotional-support dogs are technically pets, not service dogs. Hearing and service dogs are trained to perform specific tasks, but an emotional-support dog is a companion. They offer comfort and help with mental challenges like anxiety and depression. Yesterday, you said the main reason you wanted a hearing dog for Bethany was to give her an increased sense of security. I think this could be the perfect solution."

He ground his jaw. "How does it work, exactly? Would the dog help with Bethany's nightmares? Could the dog go to school with her?"

"Emotional-support dogs are often a huge help with nightmares. We'd need to get a letter of recommendation from a mental-health professional, but that wouldn't be an issue. Helping Hounds maintains relationships with several therapists who work with our clients." Ella was confident she could get a prescription for Bethany to have an emotional-support animal. Bringing the dog to school was another matter entirely. "Schools and other public spaces aren't legally obligated to admit emotional-support dogs, but rules vary from school to school. I have a feeling the principal at Snowhaven Elementary might be open to it, considering Bethany's deafness, paired with the recent loss of her only parent. Helping Hounds always participates in the school's career day, so my business partner, Willow, knows the staff quite well. Willow can be rather persuasive."

"In other words, you have no idea if she could take the dog to school," he said, somehow managing to put the most negative spin possible on what she'd just said.

"We'll have to cross the bridge when we come to it, but I would love that for Bethany. I'm prepared to help make that happen for her, so long as she can properly care for a pet on her own for the length of a school day." That remained to be seen, although from what Ella could tell, Bethany seemed like a responsible kid. Ella tipped her head in the direction of Gran's room. "She already seems pretty fond of the dog, don't you think?"

Luke's forehead creased—hardly the reaction she'd anticipated.

"You're talking about the fluffy little dog in there?" He hitched a thumb toward Gran's door.

"Yes. She's a purebred Cavalier King Charles spaniel. They're famous for their gentle, loving temperaments. They make excellent therapy dogs. I think she could really help Bethany…"

Luke held up a hand, stopping her before she could get to the part about the dog being deaf. "Hold up. As cute as that dog is, she looks like a puppy."

"She's six months old," Ella said.

Why did this conversation feel like it was going off the rails? On the plus side, the butterflies in her stomach were slowing to a standstill.

"That's a puppy," Luke said tersely. "Is she even fully house-trained?"

"I'm not sure yet. I took her home from the shelter yesterday and she spent the night with me with no potty accidents. But it's too soon to tell for certain. House-training isn't too difficult, though. At her age, it shouldn't take long at all."

Luke crossed his arms and shifted from one foot to the other. For a man who'd all but begged for a dog yesterday, he seemed remarkably unconvinced. "How do you even know she'd make a good emotional-support dog?"

"Like I said, her breed is known for bonding really well with people. Cavaliers are naturally affectionate, and I spent enough time with her last night to know she's a total lovebug." Ella took a deep breath. "Plus there's something else that makes me think she's destined for Bethany."

He frowned. "Destined? That's an interesting word choice."

"The puppy is deaf." There, she'd said it. Surely he'd understand why she was so convinced the dog belonged with his niece. "The way I see it, God is playing a big part in this."

She felt a smile blossom on her lips as she searched Luke's chiseled face for a hint of the boy she'd once known. He'd hardened in ways she couldn't quite put her finger on, but she knew the old Luke was still in there somewhere. And even though he'd never adored her in the same way she had him, he'd always been kind to her... always seemed fascinated by the way she looked for God in everyday moments, big and small. He'd shown her the tender heart beneath his rough exterior back then, and she had to believe it still beat inside his broad, grown-up chest.

His eyes, the same icy blue they'd always been, burned hot. Ella swallowed hard. "Wouldn't you agree?"

The puppy is deaf.

Luke tried to concentrate on everything Ella said next but it all felt like background noise.

A deaf puppy—one that Bethany had found at the shelter just after his visit to Helping Hounds. He could barely process it. As impossible as it seemed, he almost believed she was right. Could this be an answer to prayer?

His heart wanted to believe it so badly, but Luke's head was still snagged on all the little details that felt like red flags. He'd wanted a working hearing dog for Bethany— one that was already trained to make their lives easier. A dog that would stick by her side and know what to do, not a puppy that needed constant supervision. And how did a deaf dog even learn things? If it slipped out the door and ran into the street, he wouldn't be able to call for it to come back. The potential for disaster seemed high. He was already on shaky ground. The last thing he wanted was to make another mistake where Bethany was concerned, and this felt like it could be a big one.

"Luke?" Ella waved a hand in front of his face. "Hello? Are you listening?"

"Sorry. This is a lot to take in." He raked a hand through his hair, tugging hard at the ends.

"I really expected you to be thrilled about this." Ella regarded him through narrowed eyes until her stare turned into a glare.

He glared back. If she thought she was the only person he'd ever disappointed in his lifetime, she was sorely mistaken. "I don't know the first thing about training a deaf dog. Do you?"

"Not really, but I'm certain we can figure it out," she said, as if doing so would be the easiest thing in the world.

He arched an eyebrow. "*We?*"

Ella's cheeks flared pink. "I'd obviously help you. This is what I do for a living. I train dogs to make life easier for people with special challenges. It's my calling."

Her *calling*.

Luke wondered what it was like having one of those… What it was like to be so certain that something was a gift from God. He wished he knew.

"The puppy will go home with you, but I'll get you all sorted with the proper supplies and I can come over for daily training sessions. It will work. I know it will. This could be a game changer for Bethany," Ella said.

Two ladies pushing aluminum walkers passed them on the way to the activity room, and Luke stepped aside to make adequate space. Why did he get the feeling that he and Ella would be a hot topic among the assisted-living facility's grapevine after today?

Which begged another important question.

"How do you suppose your brother might feel about us working together like that?" Luke asked. "On a daily basis."

He didn't know if Travis had ever told Ella about what happened on graduation day. The two best friends had come to blows once Travis learned that his little sister had been writing Luke love letters. Travis blamed Luke for leading her on, even though that had never been his intention. He cared for Ella. He always had. He'd never wanted to hurt her.

Leaving Snowhaven had always been on Luke's agenda, but the fight with Travis had hastened his departure. Without Travis and without Ella, there'd been nothing left for him in Alaska.

Ella's forehead puckered. "Why would Travis even care?"

Ah, so he hadn't told her. Good to know.

"Think about what's best for Bethany, Luke. Not only would a deaf emotional-support dog make her feel less alone, it would also give her a companion that's just like her," Ella said.

She was right, and he knew it.

He sighed. "This just feels very…complicated."

He meant the part about heaping more responsibility on his plate when he already felt overwhelmed to the point of failure, but that wasn't how Ella interpreted it.

"Look. If you're worried I'm going to fall in love with you again, don't." Her flushed cheeks turned a deeper shade of crimson, and somehow, she looked lovelier than ever. "Because I promise you I'm not."

Luke almost smiled, but he didn't dare. "You sure about that, Elly Bean?"

No sooner had the words left his mouth than the truth hit him square in the chest. He wasn't worried about Ella falling for him. Quite the opposite.

They weren't kids anymore, and Ella had grown into a beautiful woman with a beautiful soul. She was throwing him a lifeline, and all he could think about at the moment was her heart-shaped face and the tender way she'd interacted with Bethany.

"I've never been more sure of anything in my life," she said in a crisp, determined voice.

Well, that settles that. A wave of something that felt too much like disappointment washed over him.

But Ella was still off-limits, right along with every other female on the planet. All Luke wanted was to build a healthy, stable home for Bethany. She was his first and only priority.

"I'm going to need some time to think about this," he said.

Translation: once you're gone, and I can see straight, I'll realize what a terrible idea this is.

Surely there was another dog out there more suitable for Bethany. He guessed the shelters were full of older, calmer dogs that might be hard of hearing. Maybe he could even find a different service-dog program willing to work with them.

Sure, and maybe you'll win an Uncle of the Year award someday, too.

Weirdly, Luke had the urge to pray for God's guidance. But he had a feeling he already knew the answer. He just didn't like it.

"Wow, okay." Hurt was written all over Ella's face. "Let me know when you make up your mind."

Then she breezed past him and reached for the door. Luke paused to collect himself, feeling like he'd been left out in the cold Alaskan snow when he heard Ella talking to Bethany in a singsong voice that the little girl would never hear. It didn't matter, though. Ella's heart shined through in everything she did. If Bethany ever drew her a picture, she'd use every pink crayon in the box.

He took a gulp of air and stepped inside the room. He slowed to a stop when his gaze landed on Bethany hugging the puppy to her chest. The smile on the child's face rivaled the dazzle of the Northern Lights in a velvety dark Alaskan sky.

Luke's eyes found Ella's.

"I thought about it," he heard himself say. "The answer is yes."

Chapter Four

Ella took the Cavalier puppy home with her for one more night to give Luke time to talk to Bethany about adopting the dog and to shop for the list of puppy supplies she gave him. She left Snowhaven Assisted Living with Luke's number saved into her phone and a promise to get together the following morning at ten o'clock for the puppy's first training session. That would give her time to do some research into training techniques for deaf dogs, as well as provide Luke a chance to puppy-proof his grandmother's cottage in town, where he and Bethany were apparently living. It all sounded like a brilliant plan...

Until Ella's doubts began to set in sometime around two in the morning.

What if he changes his mind? She gnawed on her bottom lip in the darkness. She'd been in bed for hours already and had hardly slept a wink. *What if he only pretended to agree to the arrangement to get rid of me?*

Beside her, the sweet dog's body rose and fell with the gentle rhythm of sleep. If Ella had been training the pup as a guide or assistance dog, she would've already introduced her to a crate. But since Luke had specifically mentioned Bethany's nightmares, she was hoping having the dog close at night would give the girl a sense of comfort and security. The little pup certainly seemed up for the task. She'd been stuck to Ella like glue since the moment they'd gone to bed.

Her mind just wouldn't stop spinning with ideas for different ways that an emotional-support dog could help Luke's niece. *That's* why she was so invested in this arrangement. Not because she was emotionally attached to Luke Tanner and his adorable little girl, or worse, attracted to Luke after all this time. So what if he still had the same easy charm he'd been so famous for back in high school? She'd promised she wouldn't fall for him again, and she'd meant it. She'd meant it so much that here she was, at two in the morning, cataloging all the reasons why she shouldn't—*wouldn't*—find him attractive. It was just like counting sheep, only not quite as effective when it came to getting any actual shut-eye.

Hence her giant yawn as she walked through the front door of Helping Hounds the following morning, a good fifteen minutes later than when she normally got to work.

Molly's eyes lit up the instant she arrived. "Oh, good. You're here. We were just talking about you."

"Good morning, Ella," Willow, her codirector at Helping Hounds, wiggled her fingertips in a little wave. Her guide dog, Bear, a golden retriever with a thick, honey-colored coat and the breed's trademark gentle disposition, wagged her tail in greeting but remained snug at Willow's side.

"Hey, everyone." Ella walked briskly toward the reception desk, leading Bethany's puppy on the new leash she'd introduced to the dog at home last night. "Sorry we're late."

"Your idea of late is nuts. We haven't even opened yet," Molly said with a laugh.

"I'd just hoped to get a jump on the day before things get hectic around here." Translation: before she found a dog standing on her desk and her files all over the floor. Hopefully, that was just a one-time thing.

"I hear the pitter-patter of tiny paws. Who's your new friend?" Willow tilted her head toward the puppy.

The two women had met the summer after they'd both graduated from high school at a recreational camp for visually impaired teens, where they'd worked as camp counselors. They'd become fast friends, bonded by their mutual interest in working with assistance dogs. Willow had been born with a congenital condition that caused low vision and had already had a guide dog of her own for two years, so she knew firsthand the difference a working dog could make in a person's life. Ella's father had been an avid dog musher, so she'd grown up around canines her whole life. She'd always known she wanted to work with dogs. That summer eight years ago had been the very beginning of Helping Hounds.

"She doesn't have a name quite yet, but that should change soon." Ella scooped the puppy into her arms and set her on the counter of the reception desk. "She's a little Cavalier King Charles I picked up the other day at Frosty Paws. She's deaf, and I'm pairing her with a deaf little girl as an emotional-support dog."

Willow grinned as she ran her hand over the small dog's back. "What a great idea. Sounds like a perfect match."

"Wait," Molly said as she scratched the puppy under her chin. The little dog tipped her head back and closed her eyes, clearly enjoying all the attention. "Does this have anything to do with that guy who stopped by the other day? The cute one?"

The corners of Willow's lips lifted. "Cute, huh?"

"If you're into the whole hulking-professional-athlete type." Which Ella wasn't, obviously. "He's a hockey player. Unfortunately, he's also got the personality of a grizzly bear. He just became the guardian for his niece, and she's precious. I really think an ESA could help her."

"A grumpy hockey player, a sweet little girl, and a rescue puppy. Sorry, but I agree with Molly. The word *cute* definitely applies," Willow said.

Ella cleared her throat. "Is there a reason you were talking about me just now that doesn't involve Luke Tanner?"

"Yes, actually." Molly nodded and reached for something in her top desk drawer. "I was just telling Willow about this carving I found last night near the Snack Shack. It looks just like the ones in your office."

Molly placed a small wooden carving of a moose onto the counter, and Ella's heart leaped straight to her throat the moment she set eyes on it.

She could barely form words as her breath bottled up tight in her chest. "Wh-where did you say you found that?"

"By the Snack Shack. You know—that food truck downtown with the good reindeer stew," Molly said.

Ella knew the place. Everyone in town loved the Snack Shack. She was simply having trouble wrapping her mind around a carving that looked so much like the ones her dad used to make and leave around town popping up years after he'd passed away.

"It was just sitting there on one of the picnic tables. I asked around and no one seemed to know where it came from." Molly shrugged. "Do you think it might be from the same artist who carved the others?"

"Maybe? I guess it's possible." Ella swallowed hard. Some of her earliest childhood memories involved the fresh, crisp scent of wood from the white spruce trees that surrounded the big log home where she and Travis had grown up. Dad liked to whittle in the evenings—usually small carvings of his sled dogs or other Alaskan wildlife. Instead of Barbie dolls or action figures, she'd grown up playing with her little wooden animals. Was it any wonder she'd grown up to be a dog trainer?

"My dad actually did the carvings in my office. I've had them for years. He used to make them for me and my brother when we were kids. Once we got older, he kept whittling and would leave figurines hidden around town. He liked surprising people." Ella smiled to herself at the memory of her dad, always with a pile of wood shavings at his feet when he wasn't out mushing. He'd passed away eight years ago, though. The likelihood of one of his carvings remaining unfound after all this time seemed slim at best—especially somewhere as public as the Snack Shack.

Molly pressed a hand to her heart. "Wow. I had no idea."

"Dad kept it a secret. He wanted them to be little anonymous gifts to the community." She reached for the moose carving, but couldn't bring herself to touch it. The Cavalier, however, had no such qualms. She licked the figurine, and it wobbled on its wooden paws.

"May I?" Willow asked, holding out her hand.

Molly placed the carving in her palm, and she ran her fingertips over it, brow creasing in concentration.

"Does it feel older, like it might've been carved at least eight years ago?" Ella asked. Perhaps someone who'd found one of her father's carvings a long time ago had decided to pass it forward in the same way that they'd originally come across it. Or maybe her mom or Travis had been thinking about Dad and put one of their old carvings out as an act of remembrance. The anniversary of his death was just a few weeks away.

"I don't know, Ella. I'm no expert, but I'm feeling a few rough spots. This carving feels more recent than something that was done that long ago," Willow said.

Molly's gaze shifted toward Ella. "Do you think someone else is carving Alaskan wildlife now and taking up where your dad left off?"

"After all this time?" Ella shook her head. "I can't imagine who would do that. Or why, for that matter."

Willow offered her the carving, and she forced herself to touch it. Just as Willow said, it didn't have the same worn, soft edges that the older carvings did, but it looked awfully similar to her dad's whittling—it had a similar rustic, homespun charm with a few visible knife marks here and there. There were enough details to indicate the artist had more than just a basic knowledge of Alaskan wildlife. Tiny grooves in the moose's antlers mimicked their real-life ridges. Short knife pricks on its muzzle and around its eyes perfectly captured the way a moose's fur tended to be shorter on the face than on its shaggy body. Even the grain of the wood seemed to enhance the rugged, wild look of the animal.

If it wasn't an original, it was an obvious homage.

Ella took a deep breath and curled her fingers around the chiseled wood, more confused than ever. She should probably talk to her mom and Travis before they heard about this from someone else or another mysterious carving popped up somewhere. And she would…later. First, she had to get through her upcoming training session with Luke, who suddenly wasn't the only piece of her past that had come waltzing back into her life without any warning whatsoever.

* * *

Luke's chest squeezed tight as he watched Bethany imitate the *watch-me* command that Ella had just demonstrated. Since the puppy—his niece had officially christened the dog Cupcake at the start of the training session—was deaf, Ella had explained they would use hand signals instead of verbal commands to communicate.

Just like me, Bethany had signed in response, using ASL.

If Luke hadn't been fully convinced that adopting this dog had been the right choice, that would've sealed the deal. He'd dragged Bethany to a strange new home in a strange new state, but she had a friend now—a friend who was a true kindred spirit.

Following Ella's example, Bethany held a small, bite-size treat near Cupcake's nose and then slowly moved her hand to the corner of her own right eye. As soon as the dog met her gaze, Bethany rewarded her by offering her the treat with an open palm.

"Very nice," Ella signed and then offered Bethany a high five.

Bethany beamed and slapped her hand against Ella's.

"I think Bethany's got it," Ella said, shifting her gaze toward Luke. The three of them sat cross-legged on the floor in the Helping Hounds training room in a loose circle with Cupcake situated in the middle. "Why don't you give it a shot? Cupcake is Bethany's companion, but it's a good idea for you to know how to communicate with the dog, too."

"Sure." Luke nodded. That made perfect sense, but he'd thought these sessions were for Bethany, not him.

Nerves skittered through him as he prepared to mimic the exercise. Ridiculous. Since when had the thought of letting down an eight-year-old child, a puppy with a saccharine sweet name, and a gentle yet determined dog trainer become more intimidating than taking a puck to the face?

Since always, in all honesty. When he'd been a teenager, Ella's steadfast belief in him had been a balm in the face of his father's constant disappointment. That same tender spirit that had made her so good with animals had softened his rebellious streak. Ella had made him want to do better, to *be* better.

Which made knowing that he'd broken her heart hurt all the more.

He pushed down the memory of her girlish, tearstained face on that awful night and reminded himself that what Ella Grace thought of him no longer mattered. This was about Bethany. But it was hard to shake the parallels between the past and the present. Once upon a time, Ella had made him want to be a better person, and now, Bethany made him want to be a better man.

"Don't forget," Ella prompted. "The point of this exercise is to associate eye contact with the reward. We want Cupcake to learn that good things happen when she pays close attention to the people in her life."

Luke nodded. "Got it."

She slipped him a treat from the little red pouch she kept clipped to the belt loop of her skinny jeans.

He held the morsel toward Cupcake's nose like Bethany had just done, but the pup was too fast for him. Before he could lift the treat and hold it near his eye, she plucked it from his fingers with a swipe of her pink tongue.

"Oops," Ella said and bit back a smile.

Bethany clamped a hand over her mouth to stop herself from laughing.

Luke relaxed ever so slightly. If his ineptitude could in any way help his niece experience a simple, carefree moment of childhood in the midst of her grief, he'd happily play the fool.

He ruffled the child's hair and signed, "You think that's funny, huh?"

Bethany nodded, blue eyes sparkling. Cupcake, who'd happily been the center of attention up until then, pawed at Bethany's knee.

Ella tapped her shoulder and signed, "Look! She's making eye contact. Quick, reward her with a treat."

Bethany did as she said, offering Cupcake one of the small, chewy snacks before she looked away.

"Timing is everything," Ella said with a wink. She glanced at Luke. "In dog training, we call that 'capturing.' She's essentially catching Cupcake offering a desired behavior and reinforcing it with a reward. It's a good sign that Cupcake is paying such close attention to her companion without being prompted. It means she's already learning. It also means that Bethany just might be a natural at this."

"I suppose it takes one to know one," he said with a smile.

He hadn't meant the comment to sound flirty, but the rosy hue that spread across her porcelain cheeks told him it had.

He cleared his throat. "Seriously, Ella. You were right about this entire thing. I know we're just getting started, but that much is already clear. I'm sorry I fought it at first. I'm not sure how I can properly thank you."

For a second, she looked at him like he was the same boy she'd known all those years ago. The past decade melted away like snow on a summer day. Then Bethany laughed again, and the sound seemed to pull Ella back to the present.

She sat up straighter and schooled her expression. "I'm just doing my job. You can thank me by making sure Bethany practices the techniques we're learning at home."

Luke nodded. A frown tugged at his lips. He wasn't in quite as much of a hurry as she was to leave the past where it belonged. "No problem."

"And I think it might be a good idea to have our next training session in Cupcake's new environment. Meeting here is great for focus, but it would be best for both Bethany and Cupcake to put their work to use in their everyday world."

"When did you have in mind?"

Ella screwed her lips like she was trying to remember something, but Luke had no doubt she could recite her schedule in her sleep. "Would the day after tomorrow work? The afternoon would be best for me. I have group training classes all morning that day."

Luke was scheduled to be at the rink that day. He had a mechanic coming by to give the ice resurfacing machine a badly needed tune-up, and he needed to start painting if he was going to get the place back up and running anytime soon.

Cupcake crawled into Bethany's lap and craned her furry little neck to shower his niece's face with puppy kisses, reminding him once again that this was his number-one priority. He needed to make this work on Ella's time, not his. The rink wasn't going anywhere, barring one of Alaska's frequent earthquakes. Considering the place looked like it would buckle under the force of a gentle breeze, even a minor seismic event might swallow it whole. If that happened, at least he might be able to recoup a fraction of his life savings in the insurance settlement.

He nodded and pretended he wasn't entertaining the idea of praying for a very specifically located natural disaster, free of human harm. "The day after tomorrow is fine. We'd need to meet at my workplace instead of at home, though. And that's probably just as well because until winter break is over at school, we'll be spending just as much time there as we will at home."

Ella's forehead creased. "Your workplace?"

"The old ice rink. I, um, bought it," he confessed. "Sight unseen, I might add. I saw it listed online and in a fit of nostalgia, I made an offer. It seemed like a great idea at the time."

Luke waited for her to gape at him in horror, but, of course, she didn't. She grinned from ear to ear like he'd just told her he'd taken in a stray dog who barely had a leg left to stand on instead of plunking down his entire life savings on a dubious real-estate investment.

"Luke, that's amazing," she gushed, and for a second, his hope sparked anew. Foolish, foolish hope. "Does Travis know? You two spent so much time together there as kids. He's going to flip."

He's going to flip, alright.

Luke stiffened. The mere mention of Ella's brother was a splash of glacier-cold water on his face. Whatever warm feelings remained between them after the successful training session evaporated into a crystalline fog of regret. "He doesn't. I haven't reached out to Trav quite yet. It's been a while, and I haven't been the greatest about keeping in touch."

"I'm sure he'd still love to hear from you. What was it that you guys always called yourselves when you were in middle school?" Her forehead scrunched in concentration. "Oh, I remember—the Ice Crushers."

Luke chuckled, despite himself. He hadn't thought about that silly nickname in years. They'd always dreamed of going pro together someday, but as they'd gotten older, real life set in. Luke was the only one who'd chased those boyhood dreams, and the reality hadn't quite matched up to the fantasy. He'd always thought it was because he'd never landed on a major league team. Being a journeyman player, hopping from squad to squad in the minors and playing for whoever would have him, wasn't exactly a stable existence. He'd had more good days than bad, but it was still exhausting. And more than just a little bit lonely...

Luke had gotten used to it, though. Now, it was all he knew. But he'd be lying if he said that being back in Snowhaven hadn't made him wonder how different things would've been if Travis had been along for the ride like they'd planned.

"As I recall, you called us something quite different," Luke countered.

Ella waggled her eyebrows. "The Rink Rats."

"Funny how you didn't have nearly as much trouble remembering that nickname as you did the Ice Crushers," he said with a smirk.

She gave him a soft, hesitant smile, and there it was again—that glow to her cheeks that made him want to memorize every shade of pink in her blush. He liked it when she looked at him like that—the way she used to, back before everything had gone pear-shaped.

Don't, he told himself. *Don't even think it.*

He couldn't do anything to jeopardize this arrangement. Bethany needed Ella. *He* needed her. She was simply being kind to him, because that's who she was. The last thing on her mind right now was penning him a love letter.

As if Luke needed a stroke of divine intervention to put a screeching stop to any lingering spark of attraction between them, the door to the training area flew open and the chocolate-colored dog from the other day bounded into the room.

"Snickers!" Ella cried.

Bethany's eyes widened as the Lab galloped straight toward Ella, tail whipping back and forth with glee.

"Snickers, sit," Ella said with utmost seriousness as he barreled into her lap like he was a Chihuahua instead of a fully grown retriever.

The dog thoroughly ignored the command. He licked her face with such force that she nearly toppled over.

Luke and Bethany exchanged an amused glance. Cupcake's ears swiveled to the top of her head as she watched the naughty dog with rapt interest. Luke hoped the puppy wasn't taking notes on this sort of behavior, even though it was undeniably entertaining in the present moment.

"Do you need some help there, Elly Bean?" he asked, doing his best to smother a laugh.

"No, thank you," she said primly as she scrambled to her feet. Snickers shimmied in circles around her with his big tongue lolling out of the side of his mouth. "I've got everything under control."

Luke cleared his throat. "I can see that."

"I'm afraid our time is up for today, though," she said in a tone that was all business, despite the antics of the chocolate Lab, who'd begun ping-ponging around the room like he had springs in his paws.

"Tell Ella thank you for her time," Luke signed to Bethany.

She lifted her dainty fingers to her chin, fingertips gently brushing her lips before extending outward with a deliberate motion, big blue eyes shining with sincerity.

"Thank you," she said in a quiet voice that Luke hadn't heard since before Steven's passing. Sometime during the past three months, he'd given up hope she'd ever use her speaking voice again. "I love her."

She hugged Cupcake tight.

Ella pointed at the puppy, made the sign for love, and then pointed at Bethany with a tender smile.

She loves you, too.

A bittersweet ache filled Luke's chest as he watched their interaction, the weight of the moment pressing against his ribs. He stood, fighting to steady himself, but the wave of emotion hit him harder than he expected. It had been years since he'd let himself feel this deeply. When he'd left Snowhaven, he'd left vulnerability behind and it was the one thing about Alaska that he didn't want back. Life was easier when he kept his heart locked up tight.

Like it or not, this place seemed to hold the key.

Chapter Five

"**I** didn't realize you'd be bringing a guest to family dinner, sweetheart." Ella's mother kissed her cheek and ushered her inside her childhood home, pausing to pet Snickers on the top of his smooth brown head.

"Sorry, I hope it's okay." Ella unwound her scarf from around her neck and stomped the snow from her boots on the welcome mat in the mudroom. "I think Snickers might need more exercise and stimulation than he's been getting lately at the training center. He's going through a bit of a rebellious phase."

"Oh, please. You know your brother won't mind. Dogs are always welcome here. Are you forgetting what your father did for a living?" Mom gave her a knowing look. A gentle smile hovered at the edges of her lips.

"Point taken," Ella said, but her own smile nearly wobbled off her face at the mention of her dad.

Her fingers tightened around the carved moose figurine nestled in the pocket of her puffer coat, out of sight. A full day had passed since Molly gave it to her, and still, she couldn't quite believe it was real. Nor had she brought herself to tell her mom and brother about it...

Yet.

She couldn't keep putting it off, though—especially

since tonight was their weekly family dinner. No time like the present.

Shortly after her father passed away, Mom had sat down both Ella and her brother and said she was ready to move from their semiremote log home to an apartment closer to town. Dad hadn't been active in competitive mushing for several years, but he'd never wanted to leave the sprawling log home where they'd raised a family and too many litters of Alaskan husky puppies to count. Once he was gone, Mom felt too isolated on the expansive plot of land, so she'd offered the house to Ella and Travis together to share, if they chose.

Ella loved the small, two-bedroom, one-bath home she rented in downtown Snowhaven, famous for its quaint, Queen Anne-style houses that had been built during the Gold Rush. Still, the thought of the big log house where she'd grown up sitting empty—or worse, being put up for sale—made her feel unmoored, somehow. So when Travis proposed moving in and turning their dad's old mushing trails into a recreational dogsledding business aimed at tourists, she'd been all too happy to support his vision. Mom had, too, and was touched that Travis wanted to follow in Dad's footsteps in his own special way, even if he bristled every time the mention of entering a dog sled race came up.

After Mom moved into her apartment, they kept up their weekly family-dinner tradition back at the house. Since Travis's culinary skills didn't extend much beyond mixing up protein-rich meals for his dogs, their mother usually brought something over in a Crock-Pot or casserole dish. Ella was pretty sure she smelled her favorite meal—beef stew with home-baked bread—wafting from the kitchen, warm and inviting.

"Come on in once you and Snickers get settled. Dinner is just about ready." Mom smoothed down the front of her Fair Isle sweater. Its camel-colored yarn perfectly complemented her soft brown eyes and chestnut bob.

"Thanks. We'll be right there," Ella said.

She toed off her snow boots and lined them up with the other shoes in the mudroom. Then, just as she reached for one of the towels Travis kept on hand for drying muddy paws, Snickers gave a full-body shake of his chocolate coat, sending snow flurries flying everywhere.

"Who's this?" Travis said, grinning as he leaned against the doorframe that led to the hallway. As usual, he was dressed in a plaid flannel shirt over a plain white T-shirt and worn Levi's. His feet, clad in a pair of the thick wool socks he wore for mushing, were crossed casually at the ankles.

Also as usual, his lead sled dog, Ruby, stood mere inches away. Travis had raised her from a puppy, and she was hopelessly devoted to him, whether she was guiding his sled through a thicket of snow-laden silver spruce trees, or lying on the sofa with her head propped on his thigh.

"Don't tell me you finally adopted a dog of your own," he added. "It's about time."

"This is Snickers," Ella said, wiping a clump of wet snow from her brow. "And he's not mine. He's one of our trainees."

The chocolate Lab cocked his head at Ruby, tail thumping against the smooth tile floor. The Siberian husky regarded him coolly. Her mismatched eyes—one blue and one brown—and the striking, masklike markings on her face almost made her look like a wild animal compared to the goofball retriever. But Ella knew better. There wasn't a dog on earth who got along with other canines better than Ruby did.

"And you really need to stop trying to talk me into adopting a dog. I don't need one of my own. I work with dozens of them every day," Ella said, positioning herself directly in front of her brother. That beef stew was calling her name, and he was blocking her way.

"Not the same thing." He pushed off the doorframe and ambled toward the kitchen. Ruby trotted hot on his heels. "Not even close, actually."

They'd gone round and round about this for years. Travis couldn't understand why she, of all people, didn't have her own dog. *But you love dogs*, he always said, as if that was all the convincing she needed. Then again, her brother's entire social circle consisted of canines instead of humans, so his opinion on the matter wasn't exactly objective.

"You really need to let this go. I'm around dogs all day, every day. I'd never have the time to devote to one of my own," she said, repeating the same excuses she'd given him time and time again. Snickers licked her hand, no doubt sensing her discomfort with the topic, which did nothing to bolster her argument. "Having my own dog would just be an unnecessary complication."

"Tell that to the chocolate Lab who's looking at you like you invented belly rubs and bacon." Travis tipped his head toward Snickers.

"Paying attention to his human is his job. This is just practice. One day, he'll be paired with the person he's meant to help." Ella gave a decisive nod, despite the doubts that had begun to nag at her where Snickers was concerned.

Helping Hounds had a great track record, but there

wasn't a guide-dog training program in existence with a one-hundred-percent pass rate. There were all sorts of reasons why dogs who'd been bred or rescued to be guides or assistance dogs didn't graduate from the program. When that happened, Ella usually contacted the family or individual who'd been the volunteer puppy raiser for the dog and offered them the opportunity to provide the pup a permanent home. She never considered the dogs who didn't go on to work as guides to be failures. All dogs were special. Just like people had different callings, some were meant to be assistance dogs and some were meant to be companions.

Snickers would find his way eventually. Ella had a soft spot for him, though. He was such a lovable doofus that it was hard not to. She was probably rooting for him a bit more than she should have.

Travis didn't need to know that, though. Besides, if she knew her brother, his next suggestion would probably be to try out Snickers as a sled dog since he had such a high energy level.

"Dinner smells amazing, Mom," Ella said as she got to work setting the table.

"It does," Travis agreed.

Once they were seated at the big farm table where Ella's family had eaten supper together for as long as she could remember, they joined hands and Travis gave thanks for the food. Conversation flowed quickly, with Mom chatting about the novel she'd been reading for the book club she attended every month at the bookstore downtown, and Travis telling an amusing anecdote about the latest group of tourists he'd taken out dogsledding. Ruby curled up in a snug circle on a dog bed in front of the stone fireplace with her tail tucked next to her nose. Snickers, ever the optimist, planted himself beneath the dinner table with his chin on Ella's thigh in case she dropped any food.

Ella was so distracted, she probably wouldn't have noticed if she had. She'd moved the moose carving from her coat to the pocket of her chunky knit cardigan, and it seemed to grow heavier by the minute—metaphorically speaking, of course. Her leg jiggled while she waited for an opening in the conversation. It was a wonder that poor Snickers's teeth didn't start chattering.

"I have something to show both of you," Ella finally said after Travis finished his story.

"Oh?" Her mother looked up from her plate as Ella removed the figurine from her pocket and placed it in the center of the table.

"O-o-h," Travis said, but in a much more serious tone as his gaze landed on the moose. "Um, where did you get that?"

Mom's forehead creased and she tilted her head as she studied the carving. "It looks just like one of the animal carvings your father used to whittle, but I don't remember this one."

"Molly found it a few days ago. She brought it to the training center to show it to me because it looked so much like the animal figurines in my office," Ella said.

All three of them stared at the moose for a beat without saying a word.

Travis was the first to break the silence. "Where did she find it, exactly?"

"On a picnic table by the Snack Shack."

Talk about unexpected. Snowhaven was a small town, but it still seemed like a striking coincidence that someone Ella knew had been the one to find it.

Mom reached toward the moose and picked it up, turning it over in her hands. "This isn't your father's work, but it's awfully similar."

Ella nodded. "Willow said the same thing. She said the whittling felt more recent."

"She's right. It is." Mom's gaze flitted toward the fireplace, where Dad had always sat on the raised stone hearth with his pocketknife and whatever scrap of wood he'd found most recently on the mushing trails that crisscrossed the forest surrounding the property. Her lips curved into a gentle smile, and Ella knew she was picturing him there, just like she was.

"We need to figure out who carved this," Ella said.

"Why?" A shadow of concern crossed Travis's features. "Better yet, how?"

"I don't know how, exactly. But we need to know who it was. What if there are more? Maybe this wasn't the first one. If someone is out there emulating what Dad did for the community, don't you want to know who it is?" Ella certainly did.

Travis's frown deepened, and she knew he had to agree with her. How could they possibly just forget about the moose? Ella was already holding her breath every time she left the house, wondering if she was going to stumble upon another carving somewhere.

Wondering...or hoping?

A wistfulness coursed through her, making her cheeks warm. Even though this new carving hadn't been whittled by their dad, she'd have been lying if she'd said she didn't hope there were more of them out there somewhere. She didn't even fully understand why.

"You know what this is?" Mom asked, dark eyes sparkling in the light of the fire. She placed the moose back down on the table. "It's a holy whisper."

"A holy whisper?" Ella asked, but she had a feeling she knew where her mom was headed.

"Yes, it's like a little gift from God—a reminder of your dad, just in time for the anniversary of his passing." Their mother glanced at the carving again and her gaze softened. "I don't need to know whose hands crafted this, or why they did it. But I know what it means to our family, and I know the One who meant for me to see it. The rest doesn't matter."

Ella understood…sort of. She'd felt the same divine nudge when she'd first seen the moose, and that was undoubtedly why she hoped to find more of the carvings. But her curiosity was eating away at her. Someone knew something about this figurine, and she was determined to find out who it was.

"You're not going to let this go, are you?" Travis asked, eyeing her from across the table.

"Of course not," Ella said with a shrug.

"You're like a dog with a bone. You always have been." Her brother shook his head, and his mouth curved into a lopsided smile. "Remember when you got that Easy-Bake Oven for Christmas, and I tried to tell you that a light bulb couldn't cook brownies? You used that thing every single day for months, just to prove me wrong."

"One, you *were* wrong. And two, you scarfed down those brownies like there was no tomorrow." She huffed out a breath. "Also, enough about my Easy-Bake Oven. Why does everyone keep bringing that up?"

Travis tilted his head, eyes narrowing with bewilderment. "Everyone?"

"You and Luke. I realize I'll always be younger than both of you, but news flash, we're not kids anymore." She sighed.

Maybe she was overreacting, but between the moose carving and Luke showing up out of nowhere, a tornado of feelings had been swirling inside her. Ella liked things neat, orderly, and predictable. She wasn't the same girl who'd poured out her heart in anonymous letters to the boy she'd dreamed of marrying someday when she'd been a naive fourteen-year-old. That whole episode had taught her a painful lesson about keeping her expectations in check. Then, her dad passed away just two years later, and she'd devoted every ounce of energy into her professional plans. She'd thrown herself into starting Helping Hounds because that was something she could control. Standing on her own was easy. Letting other people in... not so much.

She'd ended her last relationship two years ago as soon as her boyfriend started pressing for more. When he'd complained that she spent more time with dogs than she did with him, the decision had been easy. She hadn't shed a tear during the entire breakup speech, which probably said something about how emotionally detached she'd been in the relationship.

And that was precisely how she liked it. Ella felt like she'd been called to train dogs to help people. It had always been her dream, but she wasn't so sure that love was something she was meant to have in her life. And that was okay... Safer.

Or it had been, until Luke strolled into her office and turned back the clock.

"Luke?" Travis's jaw clenched. "As in, Luke *Tanner*?"

"Yes, obviously Luke Tanner. He still hasn't gotten in touch with you?" Ella felt herself frown. That was odd. She'd mentioned her brother to Luke once or twice, and he'd said he hadn't had a chance to reach out yet. But she would've thought he'd done so by now. He'd been back in Snowhaven for nearly a week already.

"No, but he's clearly gotten in touch with *you*," her brother said. He sounded unreasonably irked at the mention of his former best friend, but maybe he was simply feeling hurt that she'd known about Luke being back before he did.

"He just moved back to Snowhaven. His brother passed away a few months ago, and Luke is now the guardian of his eight-year-old niece." Ella told them all about Luke's initial visit to Helping Hounds, although she didn't know why she felt the need to give such a detailed summary of events. She shouldn't have to explain herself. Travis never even knew she'd written the love letters that had found their way into Luke's locker during their senior year. To her immense relief, Luke never told him. Her mortification after that whole ordeal had been excruciating enough as it was.

"Such a shame about Steven," Mom said with a shake of her head. "I didn't realize he had a daughter."

"Neither did I. She's darling, though." Ella's heart swelled at the thought of sweet little Bethany. She'd done so great with Cupcake at their training session yesterday.

"You've met his niece?" Travis asked, brow crinkling.

"Yes, I—"

He cut her off before she had a chance to elaborate.

"So you're doing it? You're training a hearing dog." Travis swallowed. "With Luke."

"No. Bethany is too young for an assistance dog." Why was he being so weird about this? Travis was into sled dogs, not guide dogs, but he was familiar enough with Helping Hounds to know the basics. "But just after he came in, I came across a rescue dog at Frosty Paws that seemed like a perfect fit. She's a Cavalier King Charles, and she's deaf, too. I'm training her to be an emotional support pet. Of course, Luke and Bethany will be doing a lot of the hands-on work themselves, so we're all working on it together. I think it will be great for Luke's niece, though. As soon as I found that dog, I just knew."

"Another holy whisper." Mom's smile turned bittersweet. "I'm glad to hear Luke's back in Snowhaven, though. His father was always so tough on him, and I know he had troubles every now and then at school. I wasn't surprised when he moved away so soon after graduation, but he must have good memories here if this is where he's chosen to raise his niece."

Travis remained quiet as a multitude of different emotions moved across his features.

"Speaking of memories, he bought the rink," Ella said, casting a meaningful glance toward her brother.

Surprise splashed across his face. "Luke bought the ice rink? But it's so run-down. They don't even have a hockey league there anymore. It's hardly been open for the past few years. Why would anyone want to buy it?"

She met her brother's gaze, the weight of the past hanging heavy between them. She wasn't sure what had happened between Travis and Luke before his friend had moved away, but she was becoming increasingly convinced something had. The mysteries were really beginning to pile up.

"Why, indeed?"

Chapter Six

Luke's to-do list was longer than his hockey stick. Every time he crossed something off, another three things popped up. And that didn't even count the regular, day-to-day routine of dealing with a child *and* a dog that was technically still a puppy, neither of which he was particularly adept at handling.

He was trying, though. Last night, he'd watched a YouTube tutorial on simple hairstyles aimed at girl dads, and this morning, he'd managed to style Bethany's hair into a passable French braid. Cupcake had finally acquiesced and begun to do her potty business outside in a small area of the backyard that he'd blocked off with white vinyl picket-fence panels that he'd gotten at the hardware store downtown. The little dog didn't seem to be a fan of the snow. Then again, Luke had spent half his life in Alaska and he wasn't exactly thrilled about shivering in the dark in the wee hours of the morning while he waited for Bethany's furry companion to take care of business, so he could relate.

He didn't dare leave the dog unattended, though. Gran's cottage was in the center of town, but this was still Alaska and Cupcake wouldn't stand a chance against a wolf or any of the other myriad wild animals the state was famous for. So there he'd stood, keeping guard over the dog while marveling over the fact that he'd committed so completely to his new role as a family man, even adding an actual white picket fence to the mix. Could he be a bigger imposter?

"How can I help you folks?" an older man in a red apron asked, rocking back and forth on his heels as Luke, Bethany, and Cupcake walked through the door of the hardware store, yet again. "Did you need more fencing supplies?"

"No, thank you." Luke pulled off his hat and gloves and tucked them into the pocket of his parka. Just like the last time they'd been to the hardware store, the staff didn't bat an eye at Cupcake. The little dog was wearing the vest that Ella had given them, embroidered with the initials ESA to identify her as an emotional-support animal, but since accommodation laws only applied to guide dogs and service animals, Luke was grateful that the businesses in town had all welcomed the puppy with open arms. So far, anyway.

"Actually, today we're here for painting supplies," Luke said. A fresh coat of paint couldn't fix everything that was wrong with the rink, but at least it would make the place look somewhat clean and new. At least that's what he hoped.

The hardware clerk escorted him to the paint section, where he chose new colors for the rink's interior—navy, white, and red. The color combination felt classic and nostalgic, which was the vibe he was going for. While the clerk mixed the numerous gallons he'd need to coat the rink's interior from top to bottom, Luke threw some paintbrushes, scrapers, drop cloths, and rollers into his basket. He could practically hear the cash register chiming in his head every time he tossed something else inside. Fixing up the rink was going to be an expensive project, and he hadn't even gotten to the ice itself yet.

He was grateful the ice-resurfacing machine was back in working order, so getting the rink in skatable condition was within the realm of possibility. But he still had the musty-smelling carpet in the lobby to deal with. Plus, most of the skates he'd found in the storage closet of the rental area were covered in rust, so he'd have to invest in new inventory.

He cringed as he handed over his credit card.

"Excuse me, you wouldn't happen to be Luke Tanner, would you?" the woman in line behind him at the register said, tilting her head with a curious smile.

"Yes," Luke said warily. He still hadn't gotten used to small-town life. Being a journeyman hockey player meant he never really stayed in one place long enough to form relationships, much less have random strangers recognize him when he was out and about.

"I'm Autumn Carmichael." She pressed a hand to her chest and her gaze flitted toward Bethany, who was busy leading Cupcake around on her leash, practicing walking with the dog in heel position like Ella had taught her to do using a treat. "I'm a teacher at Snowhaven Elementary School, and I believe your niece has been assigned to my class."

No wonder her name sounded vaguely familiar. It had been listed in the email Luke received from the registrar's office the other day.

"That's right. I'm sorry I haven't been in touch. We're still getting settled and…" He let his voice drift off, unsure how to finish that sentence.

He still wasn't sold on sending Bethany to public school. If she got bullied again, he wasn't sure what he'd do.

Then again, he didn't have much of a choice. He hadn't exactly been an honor student in grade, middle or high school. As for college, he'd never even gone. He wasn't at all qualified to homeschool anybody.

"No worries at all. We're on winter break, anyway. I just wanted to introduce myself and say how excited we all are to have Bethany join us," Miss Carmichael said.

Bethany glanced over at them, and the teacher signed the word for *hello*.

"You know ASL?" Luke asked.

She offered him a hesitant, apologetic look. "Not quite yet, but I'm learning. As soon as I found out that Bethany had been enrolled in my class, I started practicing. The rest of the class is, too. We've been learning a few basic words every day, and I want you to know that I've made a few plans to make Bethany's transition as smooth and easy as possible. She'll have a seat up front, where she can read my lips, and I've recruited a couple of my brightest students to be her study buddies. They'll share their class notes with her every day and help make her feel included in school activities."

"Wow." Luke let out a slow breath. He hadn't anticipated the school making any preparations for Bethany's arrival. Maybe dropping her off wouldn't feel as much like tossing her to the wolves as he'd anticipated. "I appreciate that. To be honest, I've been concerned about how things will go. Bethany was bullied at her other school, and she's been through a hard time recently."

"I understand." Miss Carmichael nodded. "We all know she's grieving, and I'm sure there will be more tough times ahead. Just know we're ready and excited to welcome her to school next week."

"Thank you. I appreciate that," Luke said. He wanted to believe her. He *needed* to, but he couldn't help wondering if the special accommodations for her disability might draw unwanted attention or make her feel different from the other kids.

She *was* different, though. She was special and unique and tenderhearted.

Just like Ella, he realized. No wonder the two of them had hit it off so spectacularly.

Warmth filled his chest as he glanced at Bethany. Cupcake was prancing so close beside her that the puppy kept tripping over Bethany's pink glitter sneakers. He wasn't sure if that was proper heel position, but it was awfully cute. And at least the dog seemed to be doing its job and sticking close to Bethany.

His niece's eyes flicked up as if sensing his gaze on her. She grinned, and then her attention shifted toward Autumn Carmichael, still standing beside him while she waited to pay for her items.

"Hi," the teacher signed.

"Hi," Ella signed back.

"I like your dog," Miss Carmichael said, bending down and speaking directly to Bethany so she could read her lips. "She seems very sweet, and well-behaved."

"Thank you," Bethany said in a quiet voice, signing the words at the same time. Then she gave the Cavalier's leash enough slack for the puppy to scamper over to the teacher and roll onto her back, tail wagging.

A rush of relief washed over Luke as Miss Carmichael cooed over the dog and rubbed her tummy. He even managed to convince himself that maybe someday she'd be open to the idea of Bethany bringing her companion dog to school. Ella had mentioned Helping Hounds having a good relationship with the school district, but the idea of Cupcake going to school with her had seemed like a pipe dream—just another example of Ella's eternal optimism.

Maybe she was rubbing off on him, though. Maybe a little vulnerability wasn't such a bad thing if it let in some light, some hope, along with all the uncertainty that came with feeling things again.

"Excuse me, sir." The clerk who'd helped Luke with the paint cleared his throat from behind the cash register. Sympathy flickered in his gaze, and Luke got a sinking feeling in his gut. "It seems your credit card has been declined. Perhaps you have another one I can try?"

So much for hope.

Ella arrived at the ice rink right on schedule, but as soon as she stepped inside the dank lobby, she got the distinct feeling that Luke had forgotten their appointment.

"Hello?" she called, peering out at the gleaming white oval.

The lights had been dimmed over the ice, and Luke, Bethany, and Cupcake were nowhere to be seen. The front door had been unlocked, though, so she figured they had to be around here somewhere.

She followed the curve of the wall that surrounded the ice and walked toward the concession area. It had been years since she'd been inside this building, and still, she knew it like the back of her hand.

Sure enough, the long counter where she'd ordered countless cups of hot cocoa was still there. Likewise, the antique popcorn machine stood in its usual spot behind the food counter. The vintage popper was trimmed in vibrant red with glass panels so people could watch the kernels tumble and burst into fluffy, golden popcorn. Ella had sat transfixed by that thing when she was a kid while she waited for Travis to finish hockey practice. She'd done countless hours of homework at that counter until she'd successfully begged her parents for skates of her own—pristine white leather ones with pom-poms on the laces and toe picks instead of the elongated silver blades on Travis and Luke's bulky black hockey skates. Then she'd learned to trace swirling patterns into the ice in her figure skating class that took place on one side of the rink while the hockey kids chased a puck around on the opposite end.

Her first pair of skates were probably still around in the log house somewhere. They might even be the right size for Bethany. She made a mental note to have Travis look for them.

She tore her gaze from the snack area and noticed a drop cloth and buckets of paint situated near the farthest wall of the rink. Fresh paint covered half the wall, and a roller with an extralong handle sat propped against a paint tray. Someone had to be around here somewhere.

"Luke?" she called out. "I'm here for Cupcake's training session."

Just then, the back door of the rink flew open and Luke came barreling inside with the puppy tucked into the crook of his arm. He held the door open for Bethany with his free hand, and Ella couldn't help but notice that his palm and fingers were so big that they seemed to span half the width of the door. A delicate layer of snow flurries frosted the braid in Bethany's hair, and the tip of her nose was as red as a cherry. As usual, Ella's foolish heart skipped a beat at the sight of them together—the big, protective hockey player and his tiny, feminine charge.

That child had Luke wrapped around her little finger. It was so obvious.

It was also sweet enough to make Ella go a little breathless, like she'd just taken a quick spin around the ice.

"Hey!" Luke strode toward her, closing the sizable distance between them in only a few steps. "Sorry, I lost track of time and we knew Cupcake would need to go outside before her training session."

Bethany's forehead scrunched and she corrected him in rapid sign language. "I reminded you we needed to take her out. Remember, Uncle Luke?"

Ella fought to keep a smile at bay. Little Bethany wasn't going to cut her uncle any slack, was she?

"That's right, sweetheart. Cupcake is your responsibility, and you're doing a really great job." Luke's smile went strained around the edges as his gaze met Ella's, and he added under his breath, "That makes one of us."

"Is everything okay?" she asked. "We can reschedule if this is a bad time."

Luke gave an immediate shake of his head. "Absolutely not. Bethany has been counting the minutes until this session. She's excited to show you all the hard work she and Cupcake have been doing together."

Right answer, Ella thought. He was a better dad than he thought he was, putting Bethany's needs ahead of whatever was bothering him.

What *was* bothering him, anyway? He had that same desperate look about him that she'd noticed when he first stopped by Helping Hounds a few days ago. Like he was carrying the weight of the world on his back and it was slowly becoming too much to bear.

"Super," she said, grinning at Bethany. "Then we'll get straight to work and get out of your hair."

He blinked, his eyebrows knitting together before smoothing out. "Wait, seriously? You don't need me to sit it on the training?" he asked, his voice a mix of confusion and relief.

Ella shook her head. "Not if Bethany and Cupcake are doing as well together as you say they are." She winked at the little girl and signed her next words as she said them out loud to Luke. "We've got this, don't we?"

Bethany's head bobbed up and down.

"Alright, then. I'll let you three get to it," Luke said, lowering Cupcake to the floor. The puppy wiggled to get free, but she was no match for his capable grip. Her furry paws landed on the carpet with a feather-light touch.

She scrambled straight toward Ella, which was to be expected. Dogs—Cavaliers, in particular—loved greeting newcomers when they first arrived on the scene. But like a proper emotional-support dog, Cupcake's gaze never strayed from her person. She kept an eye on Bethany the entire time Ella petted her.

"See how she's looking at you?" Ella signed. "I can tell you've been practicing the attention exercises I taught you. She's checking in with you constantly to make sure she's behaving the way you want her to."

Deaf dogs relied so much on visual cues that they paid very close attention to their guardians. Clearly, Cupcake had already started bonding with Bethany, even more so than with Luke. Her big brown eyes darted to him occasionally, but the relationship between the little girl and her dog was already blossoming.

A thrill of excitement bubbled in Ella's chest the way it always did when she knew without a doubt that she'd matched a dog with its exact right person. She'd been correct to obey that nudge she'd felt at the shelter. Cupcake belonged with Bethany.

She bit down hard on her tongue to prevent an I-told-you-so from spilling out, mainly because Luke was her client now. They no longer had the kind of relationship where she could tease him like that…no matter how much being back at the skating rink made her feel like that same starry-eyed girl on ice skates who kept falling because she couldn't keep her gaze from straying toward her brother's best friend, who was zipping around the ice like a comet streaking across the night sky.

He'd been such a natural on skates—the best player on the team. Watching Travis and Luke's hockey games had always given her such a rush of excitement. Every time Luke picked up his stick, she knew something great was about to happen. He played fast and fearless, like his whole life depended on shooting that tiny black puck into the goal. He was daring and dangerous, both on and off the ice, but never around her. Luke had always treated her with a gentleness that he rarely let anyone else see. Of course, she'd known about his bad-boy reputation, but around her, he was different. Back then, he was the only person who seemed to take her seriously when she talked about dogs and wanting to help people. He'd made her feel special. *Seen.* And when he'd first called her Elly Bean, she'd gone home from the rink that day and written a single sentence in the diary with the gilt-edged pages and tiny lock that she kept hidden under her pillow.

Someday I'm going to grow up and marry Luke Tanner.

Someone should've taken away her pen right then and there. Maybe if they had, she'd never have written him all those embarrassing love notes once she'd gotten to high school. How pathetic could a person get?

"Ella?" Luke tilted his head, watching her intently as if trying to decode the thoughts behind her quiet expression as she petted the dog. "So are we good here, then? If you don't need me, I'm going to get back to painting."

She gave the puppy's rump a pat, nudging her toward Bethany. Then she stood and crossed her arms over her chest, like a barrier. Ella didn't need Luke. She didn't need anyone. Not anymore. "We're fine. Go do whatever you need to do."

His eyes roamed over her face skeptically, as if he was trying to figure out whether she was hiding something. She swallowed hard. The only thing she was trying to hide was the fact that she'd just remembered that ridiculous diary entry.

"Okay, then." He hitched a thumb over his shoulder toward the paint tray and roller. "I'll be right over there if you need anything."

"We won't," she said a little too quickly.

His gaze lingered on her until her cheeks went warm. *Liar*, that look seemed to say. Then he turned and walked away, and inexplicably, that same pull she'd always felt for him came rushing back, stretched taut between them like a smooth satin ribbon.

She did her best to pretend it wasn't there, but for the rest of the training session, she kept finding herself searching for him across the rink, just like she had long ago. And as much as she didn't want to believe it, the pounding of her heart had nothing whatsoever to do with the crisp chill of the ice brushing against her face like a memory, frozen in time.

Chapter Seven

For the next hour, Luke somehow managed to push aside his anxiety and concentrate on painting. Physical tasks had always been his strong suit. When he'd been a kid, hockey had provided him with an escape from his troubles at school and at home. The tension in his shoulders would begin to ease the instant he laced up his skates. Out on the ice, he was capable and in control. The harder he pushed himself, the more his troubles melted away.

If he pretended hard enough, he could almost make himself believe that the paint roller in his hand was a hockey stick. He moved it around with graceful force, covering the yellowed walls and the garish graffiti tags that had been sprayed by trespassers at some point over the past few years.

Now that he'd actually looked into the rink's recent history, he'd been able to piece together its inevitable decline. It started a few years after he'd left Snowhaven, when budget cuts had put an end to the community-funded hockey league. Without the hockey kids, interest in public skating sessions dwindled. Eventually, the rink stopped renting out skates altogether and shuttered the concession stand. The only reason the neglected building still had anything resembling a half-decent patch of ice was because it was the only place within a hundred miles where young figure skaters could practice. Private lessons had ceased ages ago, but skaters still rented the facility for weekly practice sessions. And he was glad they did. He shuddered to think what kind of state he would've found the place in otherwise.

His short-term goal was to get the rink back up and running for public skating. It was the surest and quickest way to bring in some money. This morning at the hardware store had been a brutal wake-up call—so brutal, in fact, that he'd caved and called the real estate agent who'd facilitated his purchase of the rink online and asked if she knew of any other interested buyers. He'd take a loss if he had to. At least if he could pawn off the place on someone else, he'd have a little money in the bank again.

The call hadn't been promising in the slightest. Luke's offer had been the only one in the entire thirty-six months the rink had been for sale. He was officially stuck with this money pit. One way or another, he had to make it work.

"Wow, you made a lot of progress in an hour." Ella's voice caught him by surprise. Had it been an hour already?

He set down the roller and swiped his forearm against the beads of sweat that had gathered on his forehead, despite the cool breeze coming from the nearby ice. "One massive wall down, three more to go. Plus all the trim."

He'd barely made a dent.

"Don't stop on my account," Ella said with a shrug. She tipped her head toward the lobby area—a large carpeted space typically reserved for trying on skates but had recently turned into a makeshift puppy playground. Cupcake's toys were scattered all over the place, along with her food and water bowls and the crate she occupied in the rare moments when she wasn't glued to Bethany's side. "We started working on basic obedience skills today. It's important for emotional-support animals to have good manners, both at home and in public. Something tells me Bethany and Cupcake are going to be busy for a bit. Your niece is really devoted to that dog."

He looked in the direction of her gaze, eyes landing on his niece. She swept her hand in an upward motion, palm facing the sky. Cupcake immediately plopped into a sit position. "More hand signals. Looks like sign language for dogs. You've really never trained a deaf dog before?"

"Nope." Ella laughed softly, and for some reason, the gentle sound reminded Luke of the church bells that rang every hour from the little white chapel in downtown Snowhaven. "It's not that different from regular dog training, though. We typically use hand signals in conjunction with verbal commands."

"Stop downplaying it. I realize this is new to you, and you're obviously working hard to help Bethany connect with her new companion. I hope you know how much we—" his throat went tight "—*I* appreciate it. You're great at what you do, Elly Bean."

The nickname slipped out before he could swallow it down. He'd told himself to stop calling her that. She wasn't a kid anymore. Far from it. If the Ella Grace of today had offered her heart to him on a silver platter like she had back when he'd been eighteen, he wouldn't have hesitated to sweep her into his arms and kiss her.

But that would never happen. She'd promised him she wouldn't fall in love with him, and that was a good thing. His life was a mess right now. *He* was a mess, and Ella clearly had no interest in him in anything other than a professional capacity.

Still, the instant the endearment came out of his mouth, her gaze softened.

"What are you thinking right now?" he asked. Nostalgia burrowed in his chest, mixing with something warmer, deeper. "You have the same faraway look in your eye that you did when you first got here."

"Am I that obvious?" She pressed her lips together to suppress a smile. Then she sighed and looked around, gaze hovering over the frosty white ice. "I like being here. It reminds me of when we were kids. We had some great times here, you know? Me, you, and Travis."

Travis.

Was Luke ever going to set eyes on his old friend again?

He dragged a hand down his face and glanced up at the peeling paint he'd yet to deal with. More graffiti. "This isn't the same place it was then, though. I'm surprised you even recognize it."

"It's a treasure, just like it always was," she said, and her voice was laced with a wonder that made him forget, just for a moment, how much had changed in the past ten years.

But it had, as he was all too painfully aware. "Are we not looking at the same thing? This place is a dump."

She gave him a playful swat with one of her graceful hands. "Stop. It just needs a little sprucing up, and you're the perfect person to do it. You're a legend in Snowhaven—the only professional hockey player from anywhere around here. Once you open the rink back up, people will come here in droves. Mark my words. Oh, I know! You should have a grand reopening party. Invite the whole town. I bet you'd have enough kids show up to start a whole new hockey league."

Luke's eyes lingered on her like a memory. He wanted to lose himself in the way she saw the world. "You always did see the best in things that were falling apart."

"The rink isn't broken, Luke. It just needs a little tender, loving care," she said quietly.

She wasn't talking about the rink anymore, though. She was talking about him…at least that's how it felt—like he was caught in something bigger than himself. Something better.

"Ella." His breath hitched, betraying more than he intended.

They needed to talk about the past. He knew he'd hurt her, and he wanted to tell her how sorry he was. He'd handled things badly when she'd revealed herself as his secret admirer, and then he'd just disappeared from her life altogether without even saying goodbye. He owed her an explanation—or at the very least, an apology.

Some of the story wasn't his to tell, but he had to say *something*. They couldn't keep tiptoeing around the situation anymore. He'd adored her back then—not in the way she'd wanted him to, but with their age difference, that wouldn't have been right. The four years that separated them had felt like a lifetime when they were teenagers.

They weren't teenagers anymore, though—a fact that was becoming harder and harder to ignore the more time they spent together.

She'd deserved to know how special she'd been to him once upon a time.

But Ella seemed to sense the direction his thoughts were spinning as clearly as if they'd just skated right past them and twirled into a triple axel. And the fear in her eyes told him their past was the last thing in the world she wanted to talk about.

"I should get back to Helping Hounds," she said, fumbling around for her phone and glancing at the time. "There's probably a runaway chocolate Lab snoring on my desk, and I have a training class starting soon."

Sure you do.

Luke forced a smile, hoping she wouldn't see the crack in it. "Thanks again for the private session. See you the day after tomorrow?"

She blinked as if she'd forgotten they had another session booked this week, then quickly collected herself. "Yes, of course. Feel free to reach out if Bethany has any questions about what we went over today."

"Will do," Luke said. "Thanks again, Ella. You and Cupcake are making a real difference in Bethany's life. I truly mean it."

"She's a great dog," Ella said.

And you're a great person, Luke thought. But he didn't say it. He didn't dare, lest he scare her off completely.

"See you," he said instead.

"See you." She took a few backward steps and then turned around, shoulders squared.

Luke watched as she paused in the lobby to sign a goodbye to Ella and give Cupcake a final snuggle. Then she was gone, and when he redirected his attention back to all the painting he still had left to do, the walls didn't seem quite as drab as they had before. He could almost see how different they'd look once he'd finished and the colorful new trim was in place. Somewhere in the back of his head, he heard the familiar sounds of the hockey practices of his youth—the sharp scrape of blades carving into the ice, the hollow thud of a puck smacking against the boards, the muffled echo of laughter bouncing off the rink's walls.

Maybe a grand reopening party wasn't such a bad idea, after all.

The following morning, Ella sat at her desk at Helping Hounds, staring at the dog standing on top of yet another stack of behavioral-assessment reports. This most recent canine nuisance wasn't a chocolate Lab, though. In fact, it wasn't even a living, breathing animal at all. It was another carved, wooden figure, exactly like the ones her father used to whittle—and, according to what Molly had just said to her, someone had left it on one of the benches that stood directly in front of the training center.

"I can't believe this." Ella shook her head. Maybe if she shook it hard enough, she could wake herself up from this wild dream. Except it wasn't a dream at all, was it? It was her actual life, which had taken some really confusing turns lately. "I know for a fact this wasn't out front when I got here an hour ago. I would've noticed it."

The carving was about the same size as the moose that had turned up a few days ago. This one was a sled dog, with its tail curled over its back and pricked ears like a Siberian husky. In Alaska, most sled dogs were actually Alaskan huskies, not Siberians. Her father had been one of the only competitive mushers in the area who'd had a few Siberians on his team throughout the years. Ruby, Travis's lead dog, was a direct descendant of Dad's favorite, Onyx.

Which made the appearance of this latest carving even more intriguing than the last one.

"I can't see how you would've missed it. It was on the

bench closest to the walkway. I noticed it right away." Molly gestured toward the front of the building.

The exterior of Helping Hounds was used as a training area to help teach guide dogs and their handlers how to navigate around common obstacles like curbs, steps, and crosswalks. Benches were located at various points along the crisscrossed sidewalks, with the closest one situated just a few feet from the ramp leading up to the entrance of the building.

"That means whoever left it there must've done so within the past forty-five minutes. I got here an hour or so ago, and I know I would've noticed it on that bench if it had been there then." Ella gnawed on her bottom lip and absently stroked Snickers's smooth brown head. The retriever had been sprawled underneath her desk, but sat up to rest his chin on her thigh as soon as Molly revealed the little dog carving.

The receptionist was still wearing her coat, zipped up to her chin. Her handbag, an oversize tote that could fit all manner of things, including—once—a live puppy, dangled from her shoulder. Ella didn't think the receptionist had even stopped at her desk yet. She'd come running into her office with the small carving clutched in one of her mittened hands as soon as she'd arrived.

"I can't believe the mystery whittler was right here, and I missed them." Ella let out an exasperated sigh. When Snickers mirrored her behavior and let out one of his own, she couldn't help but smile, despite the bizarre turn of events.

"Do you know what I think?" Molly's eyes lit up. She still seemed a little breathless from the adrenaline of her discovery. "I think whoever is doing this *wanted* you to find it. Maybe they even wanted you to see them leave it behind."

"Then why not just come inside and introduce themselves? Why all the secrecy?" Ella sat back in her chair, eyes still glued to the wooden-dog figurine.

She couldn't bring herself to touch it yet. She felt like she was playing a game of hot potato, and no one wanted to get caught holding the figurine. Not even the artist who'd carved it in the first place.

"That's a good question, but there's no doubt in my mind that this little guy was meant for you." Molly gave the husky a nudge with the tip of her mitten. "Whoever is making these knows about your dad's carvings, and they know you work with dogs. And it's a Siberian, just like Ruby and Onyx. Maybe they left one for Travis, too. Or your mom."

That possibility hadn't even crossed Ella's mind. Clearly, she was too stunned to think straight.

She nodded resolutely. "I'll check with Travis in person. I need to stop by the house later, anyway."

She knew her old skates with the pom-poms had to be around the log house somewhere. Even if they weren't the right size for Bethany, she might want to use the pink fuzzy pom-poms on another pair. The little girl had made no secret whatsoever about pink being her favorite color, as evidenced by Cupcake's new leather collar.

"In the meantime, I'll keep an eye out for anything unusual out front. My desk has a clear view of the entrance," Molly said, finally pausing long enough to peel off her mittens and shrug out of her puffer coat.

"Thanks. I really appreciate it." Ella's foot tapped a nervous beat on the floor beneath her desk, and Snickers nudged ever closer, snuffling his nose into her side.

"What was that?" Molly asked as she stood and peered over the desk. A slow smile stretched across her lips when she spotted the chocolate Lab. "What's Snickers doing in here? Doesn't he usually stay in the kennels overnight with the rest of the dogs who are going through advanced guide-dog training?"

"Yes, he does." *When he's not sprawled on my bed next to me binge-watching rom-coms and eating popcorn.* Ella cleared her throat. That had only happened once…in a moment of weakness. She wouldn't cave like that again. Being at the rink with Luke yesterday had unlocked a lot of feelings she'd managed to keep tucked away for years, though. She'd needed an evening to decompress and reset, and somehow, allowing Snickers in on it had seemed like a good idea at the time. "I took him home last night for some extra home-based training."

"Home-based training?" Molly echoed with a tilt of her head. "We do that now?"

"Sometimes," Ella said evasively.

Molly's eyes narrowed. She looked wholly unconvinced. "There's nothing wrong with throwing in the towel if a dog isn't cut out to be an assistance dog. You say that yourself all the time."

Ella nodded. "I know."

"Snickers might be happier as someone's pet." Molly's gaze dropped to the dog, whose full weight was now pressed against Ella like the retriever was one of those cozy, weighted blankets that were supposed to help with stress and anxiety. "It sort of looks like he wants to be *your* pet."

Ella gave Snickers the *off* command, and he stretched out on the floor with a sigh. She really needed to stop indulging him. At this point, she was actively messing up his training. How had Ella let this happen?

It's happening because you're beginning to realize that refusing to let anyone get close is lonelier than you want to admit.

"He's not my pet. He's a working dog in training, and I simply have a vested interest in eradicating his naughty streak," Ella said as Snickers began to snore. Why did those snuffling noises he made sound so cute? It was supposed to be annoying.

Molly pressed her lips together like she was trying not to smile. "Or maybe you just have a soft spot for a bad boy with a heart of gold."

Luke's words from the day before came rushing right back.

You always did see the best in things that were falling apart.

Heat crept up Ella's neck, betraying her attempt to stay composed. They were talking about a dog. Not the skating rink and *definitely* not Luke Tanner.

Molly let out a soft laugh as she lingered in the doorway on the way back to her desk. "Don't look so horrified, hon. Having a gracious heart is one of the reasons you're so great at what you do. It's a good quality, not a bad one."

Was it, though?

Ella wasn't so sure. There were only so many times a heart could break, and it seemed like every loss just made hers more delicate than it had been before. That didn't feel like such a good quality. It felt pretty terrifying, honestly.

"Thank you," she said and offered her friend a watery smile. "That's a really nice thing to say."

But it didn't mean that Snickers—or anyone else—belonged with her.

The knowing smile that Molly gave her in return was disarming, as if she knew what Ella was thinking. Her gaze flitted ever so briefly to the Helping Hounds mission statement hanging on the wall and then back to Ella, eyes going impossibly soft. After she left, Ella reread the familiar words of Isaiah, even though she'd committed them to memory years ago.

And I will bring the blind by a way that they knew not; I will lead them in paths that they have not known: I will make darkness light before them, and crooked things straight.

And for the first time, she wondered when she'd stopped trusting that that sacred promise wasn't just meant for the people who came to Helping Hounds looking for an assistance dog. It was meant for all of God's children who were lost or struggling. It was meant for everyone— Ella, too.

All she had to do was believe.

Chapter Eight

"Found one!" Bethany did a little dance in her chair as she slid a puzzle piece into place at one of the four-top tables in the lobby at Snowhaven Assisted Living. Cupcake sat in her lap, content to watch intently as the humans around the table participated in the facility's weekly puzzle hour.

Gran exchanged a glance with Luke, her eyes dancing. She didn't say anything about how overjoyed she was to hear Bethany use her speaking voice. She didn't have to. Luke had expressed his concerns about his niece's unwillingness to talk several times over the past three months. She knew how worried he'd been about Bethany.

But Gran had always reminded him to wait and give things time. Bethany was grieving. Her heart simply needed the time and space to heal.

Luke knew his grandmother was right, but he also knew that time wasn't the only thing responsible for his niece's recent progress. He had Ella to thank for that. Matching Cupcake with Bethany as an emotional-support dog had been a stroke of genius. Adding a young dog to their household had been an adjustment, obviously, but the pros far outweighed the cons. So far, at least.

Was God's hand really in this, though? Ella certainly

believed it was. She'd even used the word *destiny* when she'd talked about finding the dog at the shelter. Luke wanted to agree—he wanted to so badly that he'd even begun talking to the Lord again on occasion. He hadn't prayed in so long that he wasn't sure he remembered how, but somewhere deep inside, his soul still knew. He found himself praying sometimes without even realizing he was doing it. At first, he'd tried to fight it. Why would God care about helping him now, when Luke had all but forgotten about the Lord when he'd left Snowhaven?

But the more he gave in and let himself pray, the more natural it began to feel. There were so many things about faith he still didn't understand and probably never would, but that was sort of what faith was all about, wasn't it? Believing without seeing…without knowing. That certainly fit the bill. Luke wasn't sure of *anything* at the moment…

Except that he was terrible at this puzzle business.

Bethany's forehead scrunched as he tried to force a piece in place. Each table was working on a different puzzle, and Gran had let Bethany choose theirs. She'd picked one that showed three fluffy kittens curled up by a frosted window, watching snowflakes fall outside. According to the box, the pieces were designed for seniors—extralarge for easier handling for people with arthritis or vision difficulties. Luke shuddered to think how he would've fared with a 1000-piece number instead of this "easy" version with its mere three hundred pieces.

"It goes like this, Uncle Luke," Bethany said as she slipped the cardboard puzzle piece from his fingers, turned it ninety degrees, and popped it in place as one of the kitty's noses.

In his defense, he couldn't remember the last time he'd

participated in something as wholesome as puzzle night. He had to be a little rusty.

On the hockey bus, the extracurricular activities veered more toward rebellious antics, and at times, outright trouble. The minor leagues couldn't afford to haul players around by plane, so Luke had spent years of his life on the road, traveling from city to city with twenty-two other guys on the travel squad. With sweaty gear crammed into every available nook and cranny, the interior of the bus had a distinct aroma that Luke often described as "wet dog meets gym socks." Anyone who nodded off in the middle of the day got wrapped in hockey tape and their gear taped to the ceiling. Living conditions on the bus had sometimes felt like a frat house on wheels. Luke had lived that way for so long that he'd forgotten what it felt like to do normal, family-friendly activities—yet another reason why he wasn't cut out to be the guardian of an eight-year-old little girl.

It was growing on him, though. So much so that he was questioning his decision to ever leave Snowhaven in the first place. Things were simpler here. He'd come back because he thought it was what Bethany needed, but he was beginning to wonder if it was what he'd needed, too. Why had he been in such a hurry to get out of Alaska way back when?

Because you found out that your best friend thought you were a piece of garbage, just like everyone else in town.

Right. That.

"Bethany told me she met her teacher at the hardware store the other day," Gran said.

Luke rolled his shoulders and picked up another puzzle piece. It looked no different than all the other ones in the pile that Bethany and Gran had designated as the "gray fur pile" after sorting all the pieces by color. "She did, huh?"

He glanced at his niece to see if she'd read Gran's lips. He didn't think so. The little girl's face was screwed in concentration as she surveyed the half-completed puzzle.

"She said the teacher seemed very nice." Gran's eyebrows lifted. "Does this mean everyone is excited about attending school next week?"

"The teacher was very welcoming," Luke admitted. He still had concerns. How could he not?

The bullying back in Oregon had been a problem. A big one. That's when the nightmares had started, but Bethany hadn't had one since Cupcake started sleeping with her. She'd only recently started using her speaking voice again. He didn't want to think about what might happen if the kids at her new school teased her about the way she sounded.

"I wish Cupcake could come to school with me," Bethany said in a small voice. Apparently, she'd been paying closer attention to the conversation than Luke realized.

"I know, sweetheart. Cupcake is still young. Maybe when she gets a bit older, we can look into that. Or maybe for class show-and-tell." Did schools even do that anymore? Luke felt ancient all of a sudden. "For now, we'll have to leave her at home while you're in class. I promise I'll take good care of her for you, though."

"Can she come with us when you drop me off on Monday morning?" Bethany signed. Cupcake sat up straighter and watched the rapid movements of her hands. "And when you pick me up?"

"Of course." Luke nodded.

"And can Miss Ella come, too?" Bethany placed one

hand flat on her chest and made a small, clockwise, circular motion. Luke knew that sign well. "Please?"

He let out a quiet sigh, fingers drumming against his thigh under the table. Ella was already devoting a huge amount of time to helping them. He hated to ask her for more—especially when the favor was beyond the scope of her job. Accompanying Bethany on her first day of school was something that a friend would do.

Is that what he and Ella were now? Friends?

He hadn't expected it after their initial tense meeting at Helping Hounds, but since then, Ella had become…safe. Familiar. A presence he could count on.

But was he counting on her too much? Sometimes it felt that way, especially when he wasn't altogether sure if those feelings were mutual. When he'd tried to talk to her about the past the other day, she'd all but fled.

"Sweetheart, I don't think—" He let out a quiet sigh as Bethany's face crumpled before he even finished. "Miss Ella is already doing so much for us. I…"

Luke shook his head, unable to get the rest of the words out. Bethany and Ella had formed a real bond in such a short time. His relationship with his former best friend's little sister might still be up in the air, but there was no question about how she felt about his niece. Ella had been going out of her way to help Bethany adjust to her new life since before she'd even set eyes on the child. He shouldn't be projecting her feelings about him onto Bethany. If his niece was truly his priority, he needed to put her first. If that meant setting aside his pride and asking Ella for a simple favor on his niece's behalf, then so be it.

"We'll see," Luke finally said. He didn't want to make any promises, but he'd ask. He'd have felt a lot better about it, though, if he and Ella had spent a single minute together that didn't involve Ella's job.

Bethany nodded, mollified for now. And as she toyed with another interlocking piece of the puzzle, Gran met Luke's gaze and held it. A knowing smile played on his grandmother's lips, hinting at a secret that he hadn't yet figured out. The picture on the table was starting to come together. He could make out the outlines of the three kittens and the crystalline snowflakes against the frosty windowpane, but just like his life, some pieces still didn't seem to fit.

Perhaps they were just waiting for the right hands to place them.

Ella tucked the white skates with the pink pom-poms under her arm and paused for a beat outside the door to the ice rink. An entire swarm of butterflies seemed to be doing camel spins in her stomach.

She took a deep breath and told herself she was being ridiculous. There was no reason at all she should feel nervous about dropping by to give Bethany her old skates. She and Luke had spent plenty of time together since he'd been back in Snowhaven. The initial awkwardness had passed. He was the same old Luke he'd always been.

And therein lies the problem. She huffed out a breath. It hung in the cold, Alaskan air—a little cloud of vapor. *You fell head over heels for the old Luke, remember?*

She sure had, and what an epic disaster that had been. Which was exactly why she refused to develop feelings for him again. She couldn't imagine allowing herself to lose her heart to a dog of her own, much less a man…not even if that man was Luke.

If God was trying to teach her a lesson, surely He'd

start with baby steps instead of tossing her straight into the deep end like this.

Right, because the Bible is full of examples of the Lord doing things in a small way. Never mind big splashy miracles like rainbows, turning water into wine, and calming a literal storm.

Ella took in a steadying breath. If God could calm the stormy sea, surely He could calm the storm inside of her. In her head, she knew this was true. Somewhere deep down, her heart knew it, too. But knowing it and acting on it were two different things. She just wasn't ready to put her heart on the line. She might *never* be ready.

Her visit to her brother's house last night hadn't helped matters. Travis had seemed much more interested in why she wanted to find her old skates than talking about the dog carving. When she'd admitted that she wanted the skates for Bethany, he'd gone quiet. Travis had always been the strong, silent type, and dragging information out of him when he didn't feel like talking was an exercise in futility. She'd left the family log cabin with more questions swirling in her head than when she'd arrived, and shockingly, the most pressing ones weren't at all related to the mystery whittler. Like, why had she been so hesitant to tell Travis why she was looking for her childhood skates?

Ella didn't want to think too hard on the answer to that question. She was simply doing a nice thing. Those skates weren't doing anyone any good tucked away at the back of her old closet. Giving them to Luke's niece didn't have to mean anything. It certainly didn't mean she'd developed a soft spot for anyone, least of all a bad boy with a heart of gold.

Molly meant Snickers, not Luke, Ella reminded herself as her face went hot enough to melt the snow flurries whirling against her cheeks.

She set down the skates on the ground, propped against the glass door to the rink. The entrance to the building was covered with an overhang so they were safe from the snowfall. Luke would probably find them soon, anyway, so there was really no reason for her to stay. She had work to do—dogs to train, an unsolved mystery to figure out, an irritating brother to deal with…

Her own grown-up pair of skates were nestled in the trunk of her car, but no one needed to know about that. She'd tossed them in at the last minute, just in case Luke invited her to take a spin around the ice while Bethany tried out the skates. Although, why would he? Like she'd told Travis last night, the only reason she and Luke were spending time together was to train Cupcake. The last time Ella checked, puppy training didn't involve ice skating.

Besides, it had been years since Ella had slipped her feet into a pair of skates. She'd probably fall on her first turn around the rink. Just what she needed—another opportunity to embarrass herself in front of her one-time crush.

She gave the skates a final, protective pat and then turned to walk back to her car.

"Going somewhere?"

Luke's deep voice stopped her in her tracks. There went those annoying butterflies again. Apparently, they hadn't gotten the memo about Ella not having feelings for Luke anymore.

She squared her shoulders and turned to face him. When she saw the way he was looking at her old skates—now nestled gently in the crook of his elbow like he'd just stumbled upon a long, lost treasure—the iceberg surrounding her heart melted around the edges, warmth creeping in.

"I was just dropping those off on the way to work." She blinked against a fresh wave of snowflakes, dancing like tiny ballerinas in the frosty morning air. "They're my old ones from when I was her age."

He looked up from the skates, and when his gaze met hers, the tenderness in her eyes made her breath catch. "I remember."

She nodded and tried not to think about what else he remembered. "I don't know if they'll fit, but you mentioned the skates here weren't in the best shape and I wasn't sure if you'd had a chance to buy her a pair of her own yet."

He blew out a breath and shook his head. That tortured look was back in his eyes again, and Ella knew there was no use going back to her car. She was staying, whether he wanted her to or not.

"I wish I could." He tucked the skates more firmly under his arm. "Unfortunately, until this place starts bringing in some money, things are a little tight around here."

So, on top of losing his brother, leaving hockey, and upending his entire life to raise his grief-stricken niece, Luke was having money troubles? No wonder he'd seemed so overwhelmed.

"I sunk almost everything I had into the rink without realizing it hadn't been operational in a while. I've spent nearly all I had left trying to get it back up and running." He shot her a wry, almost apologetic look. "Dumb, I know."

She hated when he talked about himself that way. Always had. When they'd been in school, every time he'd surprised himself and done well on a report card, his brother had bettered him and brought home straight A's. Steven had been known as the smart brother, while Luke had been the hockey jock.

"Don't say that," she said, probably a little too earnestly. Ella had always been the first one to jump to Luke's defense when anyone compared him unfavorably to his brother. Some things never changed, apparently. "I love that you bought this place."

One corner of his mouth hitched up. "I know you do, Elly Bean."

She didn't mind the nickname so much this time. The past hadn't been perfect, by any means, but it had its good parts, too. Those moments had been sweet enough to make Ella want to stay and build a life here. They'd called Luke home. How could she possibly want to wish them all away?

"You're going to return the rink to its former glory in no time. I'll help you," she said, as if she needed to heap one more thing onto her plate. He looked ready to object, so she jumped in with another suggestion before he could. "But right now, I think we should skate."

He blinked at her, surprise flicking into curiosity. "You what?"

She hitched a thumb over her shoulder toward her car. "My skates are in the trunk, and you seem like you could use a break. Bethany could give my old ones a try…"

She let her voice drift off, feeling ridiculous all of a sudden. The poor guy was probably in the middle of painting or something. "Never mind. I'm sure you don't have time—"

"Are you kidding? I've always got time for a few laps around the ice," he said, mouth curving into a gentle smile.

"So that's a yes?" A warm, fuzzy feeling bloomed in her chest, despite the cold.

He winked at her, and just like that, the confident charmer was back. "That's *definitely* a yes."

Chapter Nine

"Let's see if these fit, shall we, Cinderella?" Luke signed as Bethany beamed up at him from one of the changing benches in the rink's lobby. It took him a while to spell *Cinderella* with his fingers, but the effort was worth it because when he finished, he was rewarded with a stream of giggles from the little girl.

The instant she'd spotted the pretty white skates with the bubblegum-pink pom-poms, her eyes had nearly bugged clear out of her head. Luke had checked the size stamped onto the inside of the boots before he'd shown them to her because he knew once she got a look at them, she'd have insisted on wearing them regardless of whether or not they fit. Happily, they were only a half size bigger than the shabby rentals she'd been teetering around in for the past few days.

Nothing that a nice thick pair of socks couldn't fix. At least this way, she'd be able to wear them for a good long while.

"Would you look at that?" Ella said. She sat beside Bethany, already laced up and ready to go with Cupcake nestled in her arms, as Luke kneeled down to weave Bethany's laces through the eyelets, securing them with a final tug and tying them into a bow. "They look like a perfect fit."

Luke pressed his fingers along each boot, ensuring the leather was snug against the child's dainty foot. "They sure do."

Ella held her hand up for a high five, and Bethany smacked her palm against it.

"Give me a sec to get Cupcake settled in her crate and get my skates on, and we'll give them a whirl out on the ice. Okay, kiddo?" Luke said as he stood.

Bethany's head bobbed up and down in a nod. Ella pressed a kiss to the top of the small dog's head and then handed over the Cavalier. A tug that felt an awful lot like envy pulled at his heartstrings.

Great. He was jealous of a dog now. How low could he possibly get?

"I'll be right back." He tucked the pup under his arm and went to put her in her crate in the small office off the lobby for some quiet time, like Ella had taught them to do, grateful for a moment to get his wits about himself.

Ella is here for Bethany, not you, he silently insisted, once again, as he got the dog tucked into her kennel with a chew bone and grabbed his skates.

But this time, Luke wasn't so sure that was the truth. Sure, she'd shown up with skates for his niece. But then she'd offered to help him fix up the rink, and before he'd had a chance to balk, she said she wanted to skate together. Unspoken memories had floated between them, swirling with the snow flurries—simpler days of tracing endless loops under the glow of the old rink's lights. Hot cocoa warming his hands after tugging off his hockey gloves. The way Ella had twirled so effortlessly across the ice, a smooth waltz to his furious drive.

The unspoiled innocence of childhood before every-thing had gotten so complicated.

Luke couldn't have said no if he'd tried.

He shoved his feet into his skates and laced them up quickly, fingers moving on autopilot. His skates were made for hockey, so they were stiffer than Bethany's and Ella's, with shorter, curved blades designed for fast, aggressive movements and sudden stops. But once the three of them stepped onto the ice—Luke and Ella on either side of Bethany, all three holding hands—the gentleness of the moment settled over him. His feet moved in slow, steady strokes, and his breath slowed. With each exhale, the tension he'd been holding on to so tightly lifted from his shoulders. Heat spread down his legs, but not the fiery kind that propelled him forward when chasing after a puck. This warmth was different. Steady…sure. And for the first time in as long as he could remember, he simply *was*. No worries, no doubts—only a quiet sense of peace settling deep in his bones.

They made two loops around the rink, Bethany's short strokes growing smoother and more fluid with each length of the oval. Her grip on Luke's fingertips loosened as she gradually let go of her fear of falling and grew more confident. Then she tugged her hands free and pushed forward, blades scraping softly against the surface of the ice.

She signed at Luke. "I want to try by myself now."

He glanced at Ella, and she gave him a small nod, encouraging him to let the child go. He knew he was over-protective. After all, when he'd been Bethany's age, he'd been whipping around this rink, crashing into the boards like a maniac. He was new to this, though—new to being a parent, new to grief, new to helping a child with special needs. New to all of it.

He nodded, signing an answer to Bethany as she grinned at him with an upturned face, her button nose pink from the cold. "Okay, but take it slow. We're here."

Her smile widened and she glided farther away, stumbling for a moment before righting herself.

Ella grabbed his hand and squeezed it tight to prevent him from skating over and helping her. "She's got this. She's a natural. How could she not be, with you as her uncle?"

Luke let out a low laugh. Steven had been too busy with academics to get into hockey when they were kids. He'd learned to skate in group lessons when they were really young, and that had been it. Luke was the only true rink rat in the family. "You think?"

"Of course. It's in her blood." She shook her head and gave him a sideways glance as they started skating together again, hand in hand.

Neither of them seemed ready to let go.

"You're doing great out here, by the way," he said. She had a quiet grace to her movements, same as always. "How often do you skate?"

"Not often at all. Once a year, maybe, when the pond near the town center freezes over and they open it up for skating in the week leading up to Christmas." She laughed softly, sounded a little breathless. "This feels good, though—like my body remembers this, even if my mind doesn't."

They skated in smooth circles, inching closer and closer to the center of the ice while Bethany stayed near the boards, face screwed with determination as she plowed forward. Frost coated the pom-poms on her skates.

"When you were off getting your skates and putting Cupcake in her kennel, Bethany asked me if I'd come with you Monday morning to drop her off for her first day of school at Snowhaven Elementary," Ella said, eyes fixed on his niece.

"She beat me to the punch, I guess." Luke laughed under his breath. Bethany was more headstrong and confident than he realized sometimes. That had to be a good thing, though. "I promised her I'd ask you. Please don't feel obligated."

"Stop." She gave him a playful shove, and he winced in mock pain as he encircled her with a slow spin, even as their hands remained linked. "I already told her I'd be there, and, of course, I don't feel obligated. I can think for myself, you know."

"Believe me, Elly Bean. I'm fully aware of how grown up you are. You don't have to keep reminding me." Luke laughed under his breath, but in the next heartbeat, he felt his smile fade. He wasn't teasing. He was dead serious.

Luke didn't want Ella to think he still saw her as Travis's kid sister. That wasn't the case anymore—not even a little.

"Just so we're clear, I'm here because I want to be here. I adore Bethany," she said as her eyes locked onto his. She took hold of his other hand and they kept spinning on the ice, face-to-face, turning…turning…turning, until the world around them blurred into a soft white haze. "And you're not too terrible yourself, Luke Tanner."

Warmth curled through him despite the icy air. He couldn't imagine the vulnerability it took for her to say something like that to him after the way he'd succinctly rejected her after she'd handed him her final love note. It had happened the night before his graduation, and when Ella had shown up on his front porch, he'd initially thought she was looking for Travis. Then, as he'd taken in her wide eyes and the way she'd fidgeted with her mittens, he'd thought maybe she was in some sort of trouble and needed his help. Bile had risen up the back of his throat.

Please don't let this be about a boy, he'd thought. *If someone hurt Elly Bean, I'll kill him.*

But no sooner had the thought crystallized in his mind than she'd pulled an envelope from the inside of her rabbit fur coat—an envelope he recognized on the spot as an exact match for the ones he'd been finding in his locker for months. Robin's-egg-blue, with his name written neatly on the front in loopy cursive writing. Her hand shook as she handed it to him, and she may as well have been offering him her heart instead of a girlish love letter.

"Oh, Elly Bean," he'd said. "No."

The way her face had fallen had been a knife straight to his heart. He'd cared about Ella…of course, he had. But she'd been only fourteen—a freshman—while his cap and gown hung in his bedroom, ready for the ceremony the following day. More importantly, she was Travis's little sister. There wasn't a world in which reciprocating her feelings would've been anywhere close to acceptable. Luke hadn't been perfect back then, but he'd never gone that far astray.

"But I love you," she'd insisted as tears spilled down her face.

"No," he'd said firmly. "You don't."

"Yes, I do, Luke. I always have."

The way her eyes had glittered with sincerity had just about killed him. He'd always admired her earnestness, and the last thing he wanted was to break her heart. But he'd been panicked, so he'd said the only thing he'd known for certain would make her stop.

"You don't know what love is yet. It's only a crush," he'd said.

He'd infused as much tenderness into his tone as he could manage. But hope—endless, innocent hope—still sparkled in her soft, doe-brown eyes, and he'd known then and there that sugarcoating things simply wasn't going to work.

"You're just a kid, Ella," he'd finally said, sharper than he wanted to.

That had done the trick. She'd looked at him as if he'd slapped her, and in that moment, Luke realized his worst fears had come true—a boy had indeed hurt her.

And that boy was him.

It wasn't until after she'd fled that he'd thought of a million ways he could've let her down gently. A million things he could've said.

I care about you a lot, but not in the way you're hoping.

You've got so much ahead of you—your heart is going to have so many opportunities to love.

I'm not the right person to make you feel the way you want to feel.

Instead, he'd minimized her feelings and called her a child, and it had been the last conversation they'd ever had...

Until he'd returned to Snowhaven earlier this month and turned up in her office, begging for help.

You're not too terrible yourself, Luke Tanner.

Only Luke knew how much that sentiment must've cost her. He squeezed her hands tight as the words sank deep into his chest. A ghost of a smile danced on her lips, and beneath the flirty banter, he knew there was something more happening between them. She wasn't the same awestruck girl who'd stood on his porch that snowy night all those years ago, the girl he'd known forever. She was someone new now. Someone special.

Someone he might fall for someday, if he hadn't already.

He snuck a peek across the rink at Bethany, stroking over the ice with one hand holding on to the boards and a giddy expression on her face. His niece was as content as could be. So much had changed since they'd moved to Snowhaven, but he knew the shift was more than just geography.

You're not too terrible yourself, Luke Tanner. Those words would be echoing in his head for quite some time.

Luke's skates scraped against the ice. The diamond-edged circle he and Ella had been carving together had grown so small that they were now only inches apart, breath commingling in the frosty air. He smiled into Ella's eyes, sparkling under the lights of the rink.

"You're anything but terrible, Ella Grace."

He was going to kiss her.

Ella wasn't sure how she knew for certain, but she could just sense it. And she couldn't think of a single reason why he shouldn't.

She'd wanted this for so long, but it didn't feel at all the way she thought it would. And why would it? This wasn't yesterday. This was here and now—a very real and very different present. When she looked into Luke's eyes, she no longer saw the boy she'd once idolized. She saw a man who'd lived an entire lifetime in the past decade. Those years had changed him, but here on this ice, where they shared so much history, she had a new appreciation for the myriad ways in which he was different. He was more humble than he used to be. More thoughtful. And there was a new strength to his stance—a determination to fight for the things that mattered most. Even so, underneath it all, there was still a tenderness reserved just for her.

She'd promised she wouldn't fall in love with him again, but that promise was the furthest thing from her mind as he pressed his forehead against hers, gaze dropping to her mouth. Her breath caught in her throat. Then Luke whispered her name, his voice sweet and lovely, and Ella had never felt so beautiful—so *seen*—in her entire life.

She tipped her face toward his. Her heart skipped a beat as he lowered his mouth to hers. Then, in the soft moment just before their lips touched, a loud bang echoed through the rink.

Ella felt Luke jerk away before she could process the sound. She stumbled in her skates, caught off guard by his sudden withdrawal. She pressed a hand to her chest as she righted herself and felt her heart fluttering furiously against her palm. Beside her, Luke went pale, his chiseled face as white as the ice beneath their feet, attention fixed on something over her shoulder.

Ella moved her skates into a simple, two-footed turn and followed his line of sight toward the lobby. Only then did she recognize the sudden noise as the slamming of a door as she spotted her brother standing at the entrance to the rink, gaze glued to her and Luke in the center of the ice.

Chapter Ten

"Travis, hey there." Luke did his best to pretend that he hadn't been mere seconds away from kissing his former best friend's little sister, but it was no use. The stormy expression on Travis's face said it all. He'd seen everything. "It's been a while."

Travis nodded slowly but said nothing. He just kept standing on the opposite side of the boards with his arms crossed over his chest and that terrible look of betrayal on his face. Of all the moments for him to show up out of the blue, he'd chosen the absolute worst.

"Finally," Ella said, tucking a loose strand of hair behind her ear. Her spine was ramrod-straight and her jaw set, as if she could erase the past five seconds from everyone's memory by pretending they'd never happened. "I wondered if you'd ever get out here to say hi to Luke."

Luke shifted awkwardly from foot to foot. He needed to talk to Travis alone. He needed to explain and maybe even apologize—although, he wasn't entirely sure what for. He and Ella hadn't done anything wrong. Not now, and not back in high school. Travis's interpretation of that excruciating event had never been accurate, and from what Luke could tell, he and Ella had never discussed it. By all appearances, Travis still thought Luke had somehow taken advantage of Ella's young, impressionable heart.

And whose fault is that?

Once again, Luke's decision to abruptly leave Snowhaven a decade ago had caught up with him. Back then, he'd told himself he was focusing on the future. He was leaving home and building a life, just like any other eighteen-year-old.

Deep down he'd known better. He just hadn't wanted to face it. He'd always felt like a disappointment to his parents, and his struggles in school hadn't helped. *Everyone* wanted him to be like Steven, the golden child. No matter how many times Gran stood up for him, Dad insisted he was wasting his life on sports when he should be focusing on academics. The only places he'd ever felt like he belonged were the rink and the log cabin in the woods where the Graces lived. And in one fell swoop, even that had changed.

Travis had aged over the past decade, just like Luke and Ella had. But the expression he wore as he stood in the rink's lobby was eerily similar to the one he'd had on graduation day. Luke felt like he was about to relive that painful argument all over again.

Luke had never taken that last blue envelope from Ella. He'd never read whatever she'd written inside, but Travis had. From what Luke had gathered, Ella dropped her final love letter at home somewhere after she'd fled their awkward conversation the night before and her brother had found it. After Travis opened it, he'd wasted no time at all jumping to every wrong conclusion in the book.

It's not what you think.

That was it—the full extent of Luke's explanation. He hadn't wanted to say more because he didn't want to embarrass Ella. She'd been hurt enough already. Luke had never told Travis about his secret admirer. The letters had been so personal. It hadn't felt right to share them with anyone, even though their author remained a mystery. Without that backstory, it was all but impossible to defend himself.

That was the thing, though—Luke hadn't realized he needed to defend himself. Not to Travis. Not to his best friend. Travis knew Luke better than anyone else in the whole world. He'd honestly thought those five simple words would suffice.

It's not what you think.

They hadn't sufficed, obviously. They hadn't made so much as a dent in Travis's anger, and with every accusation his friend hurled at him, Luke died just a little bit more inside. He'd convinced himself that packing up and leaving had been the honorable thing to do, but deep down he knew better. Real friends didn't just disappear. They stayed and worked through the hard stuff. In the end, Luke had given up on Travis just as easily as Travis had given up on him.

"Well, aren't you going to say hello back?" Ella arched an irritated eyebrow at her brother.

Travis gave a slow nod. The set of his jaw looked as hard as granite. "Hello, Luke."

Bethany chose that moment to skate over to Luke and crash into his legs. He planted his hands on her shoulders as she spun to face Travis and signed a greeting.

"This is my niece, Bethany." Luke gave her shoulders a squeeze and then spelled out Travis's name for her with his fingers.

"Mr. Travis is Miss Ella's brother," he signed and spoke

aloud at the same time, and then took a deep breath and continued, "He's also my friend. A *good* friend."

Travis's throat cleared. Then he offered Bethany a smile that didn't quite reach his eyes and held his hand up in a wave. "Hi, Bethany. It's nice to meet you."

"Do you want to see my dog, Mr. Travis?" Bethany said, using her speaking voice again, enunciating each syllable with care. "Her name is Cupcake."

"Absolutely. I love dogs." Travis's grin widened, and Luke got a fleeting glimpse of what life could be like if he and Bethany had friends and a support system beyond just his grandmother.

"Why don't you and I get our skates off and go get Cupcake so she can meet Travis?" Ella skated toward Bethany with her hand extended. "How does that sound?"

"Good," Bethany nodded, and she planted her hand in Ella's palm.

"Thanks, Ella," Luke said, imploring her to look at him. He didn't like the way their time together had just ended. They'd nearly kissed, and the moment he'd realized her brother was watching, he'd skated backward so fast that he'd nearly tripped over his blades. Shame coursed through him at the memory. If only it had been someone else… Anyone but Travis.

Ella didn't cast a single glance in Luke's direction. She just kept that same fixed smile glued to her face, and when she glided past him, the frosty chill that emanated from her could've kept the rink frozen for months without any help whatsoever from the pipes that ran beneath the ice.

Luke dragged a hand through his hair and skated toward the boards where Travis stood, surveying his surroundings along the way. Moments before, when he'd been skating hand in hand with Ella and Bethany, he'd been able to see the rink through a different lens. He'd seen it the way Ella did—not like it looked back in its glory days, but carefully restored to something new. A place that honored the past and celebrated the future, all at the same time, where a whole new generation could chase their dreams, just like Luke had when he'd been a kid. The rink had felt like his home back then, and he hadn't quite realized until today that that's why he'd jumped at the chance to buy it. He'd wanted to find that home again and share it with Bethany. It was the closest thing to a real home he could offer.

Now that he was looking at the rink through Travis's eyes, Luke didn't see it that way anymore. The place was a mess. Walls were half-painted and drop cloths covered most of the floor. Wires hung from the ceiling from his latest attempt to get the sound system up and running. He'd removed the cracked and scratched Plexiglas from the top of the boards, and the new sheets sat stacked in a pile, waiting to be installed. He'd set a goal date for the grand reopening party just eight days from now, mainly out of financial necessity. But progress was slow, especially since he was doing everything on his own. At the rate things were going, his goal date was nothing but a pipe dream.

"I'm glad you came," he said to his old friend when he reached the boards. Now that Ella and Bethany had disappeared, Travis had gone back to staring daggers at him.

"Yeah?" he said with a dubious look.

Luke nodded. "Yeah."

"Ella kept asking when I was going to see you. I didn't realize you two…"

Luke shook his head. "It's not what you think."

He hadn't meant to echo those same words, but they spilled out of his mouth before he could stop them.

Travis's eyes flashed. Clearly he recognized the sentiment. "I've heard that before."

"It was *never* like that between Ella and me. You have my word," Luke said quietly, lest Ella overhear their exchange.

They were going to have to talk about the past eventually, but he really didn't want to have to do it in front of her brother.

"Then why did you leave town the way you did? You just disappeared," Travis said, and Luke spied a flicker of hurt beneath the resentment in his expression.

Because I thought you didn't want me around anymore. Because if you believed the worst about me, then maybe that meant it was true. Maybe I really was as useless as everyone seemed to think.

"Because I was an idiot," Luke said, figuring that encompassed all the reasons he couldn't seem to articulate.

The corners of Travis's mouth inched upward. Just a little…just enough for Luke to remember how to breathe.

His eyes narrowed as his mouth went flat again. "I'm still not sure I believe you, given what I just walked in on."

Luke had no idea how to address the near kiss. He shouldn't have to, given the fact that they were adults now.

"Believe me, or don't. Nothing happened between us back then. She was *fourteen*, Trav. You guys were like family to me." Luke's throat went thick, and to his utter mortification, he thought he might break down in tears.

He blinked hard and looked away, toward Ella and Bethany unlacing their skates in his office. They'd already let Cupcake out of her crate, and the little dog pranced around them, pawing at the laces and biting the pink pom-poms on Bethany's skates. His niece giggled, and her laughter was a balm to his soul.

She was the reason he'd come back. Confronting his past was unavoidable, and maybe that was a good thing. Maybe everything that had happened since he'd moved to Snowhaven truly was part of God's plan. If so, he'd just have to trust that it was for the best.

He turned back toward Travis and met his friend's gaze full-on. "Anyway, like I said, I've missed you."

Travis looked at him long and hard but stopped short of echoing the sentiment. Then he let his gaze wander over the rink's interior and shook his head. "I can't believe you really bought this place."

That makes two of us. "It might send me straight to the poor house, but I'm starting to think it might be worth it."

At last, his old friend cracked a smile at him. "You haven't changed a bit, have you? Tell me—are those skates permanently attached to your feet at this point?"

Luke looked him up and down. Travis wasn't a professional athlete like he was, but he'd clearly kept himself in decent shape over the years. He was tall and broad-shouldered enough to pass for a hockey player himself. "When was the last time you got out on the ice?"

Travis laughed under his breath. "It's been a while. I mostly stick to dog mushing these days."

"That's too bad." Luke shifted his skates, gliding them back and forth as he adjusted his stance.

Travis's eyes narrowed. "Why's that?"

"I was just thinking." Luke shrugged, a slow grin pulling at his lips. "It might be fun to settle things the old-fashioned way."

* * *

"What's the first thing we should do now that we've let Cupcake out of her kennel?" Ella signed.

She and Bethany had just removed their skates in Luke's office, and Ella had wiped the blades down with a soft, dry towel while Bethany doted on her dog. Hunter at Frosty Paws had told her from the start that the Cavalier had excellent crate manners, and he'd been right. Cupcake tolerated being kenneled like a pro, but it was clear from the effusive reunion that the dog was happiest when she was with her person.

"We should take her outside for a walk," Bethany said. As soon as Cupcake made eye contact with her, she rewarded the pup for paying attention and then clipped her leash onto her collar.

"Great job!" Ella said and flashed her a double thumbs-up.

This wasn't an official training session, but it was as good an opportunity as any to reinforce some of the things she'd been teaching Luke's niece. They were doing great so far with basic obedience commands and good dog manners. At their next session, Ella planned on introducing them to deep-pressure therapy, a way for dogs to help alleviate anxiety in their handlers by applying gentle pressure to the person's body. Dogs who were highly attuned to their owners were usually great at instinctually picking up on telltale signs of anxiety, like a rapid heartbeat, shallow breathing or tears. Emotional-support animals could be taught to put their body weight on their person's lap and abdomen to help calm them down. Larger dogs were often trained to lean against their handlers, but Cupcake was the perfect size to snuggle in Bethany's lap.

For right now, though, the Cavalier only needed a

chance to empty her bladder before meeting a new friend. As eager as Bethany was to show off her dog, Ella was especially glad she remembered to put the dog's needs first.

Travis and Luke looked awfully serious on the other side of the rink as Ella and Bethany walked toward the door, bundled up in puffer coats. Cupcake wore her official ESA training vest, and her feathery tail swished back and forth with each step. Ella kept her gaze glued to Bethany and her dog. In her head, she went over the exercises she wanted to introduce at their next training session. There were ways to teach a dog to recognize emotional distress. Ella would need to talk to Bethany and Luke to figure out how the little girl's anxiety usually manifested itself when she was feeling stressed.

She bit down on her bottom lip and sank into her puffer coat as she watched Bethany walk Cupcake in the relief area Luke had set up next to the rink. Snow crunched beneath the child's boots, and snow clung to the Cavalier's feathered coat, dotting her black markings with lacy bits of white. They were making great progress. Ella needed to relax. The only reason she was writing up a training plan in her head at the moment was to distract herself from the kiss. Or rather, the *non*-kiss.

Did a kiss really count if it lasted less than a nanosecond and their lips never even touched?

No, it did not—especially if one of the parties jerked away like he'd been electrocuted the second someone else walked into the room.

Travis turning up out of the blue had been a surprise, but had it really been necessary to skate away from her so fast, like the mere act of standing beside her might get him into trouble? It wasn't like they'd actually done anything. Technically, they hadn't even kissed. Would it have been so terrible if they had? She was a full-grown adult now. She could kiss whomever she wanted, thank you very much.

Unfortunately, she wanted to kiss Luke Tanner.

Well, she wouldn't be making that mistake again. *Ever.*

Mortification curled in the pit of her stomach. How had she let this happen? Had she learned nothing the last time she'd lost her heart to Luke? She'd promised herself—and *him*—that she wouldn't fall in love with him again. At least she hadn't told him she had feelings for him. Although, it had been heavily implied.

Kissing meant something to Ella.

She should've never listened to Molly's bad-boy-with-a-heart-of-gold speech. One little crack in her resistance, and he'd swooped right in.

Like a cockroach, she thought as a fresh round of humiliation made her face prickle with heat. Except Alaska didn't have cockroaches. They had wild things like bears and moose and reindeer...

And hockey-playing men who looked like lumberjacks and could sweep a girl right off her skates.

"Miss Ella?" Bethany signed. The rapid movement of her hands pulled Ella out of her trance.

She pasted on a smile, or at least she tried. "Yes, honey?"

"Why do you look so sad?" Her sweet little mouth curved into a pout.

In ASL, the word for *sad* was a literal sad face, with the added emphasis of holding both hands in front of your face and drawing them downward. Ella wanted to kick herself. Was that what she actually looked like right now?

"I'm not sad," she signed back. "I promise."

I'm just mad at myself, that's all. And *at your charming uncle.*

She kneeled down to Bethany's level to make eye contact with the child and gave her chin an affectionate tweak. "You're right, though. I was just thinking too hard about something. My face probably does look funny right now."

Ella made a goofy expression and stuck out her tongue. Bethany laughed, and her scrunched forehead smoothed as her concern lifted.

Ella pulled her in for a hug, then signed again, fingers moving with careful precision. "I'm fine. Thank you for checking on me, though. You always know how to make me smile."

The little girl's face lit up, as bright and beautiful as an aurora-swept sky.

"Are you and Cupcake ready to go back inside?" Ella tipped her head toward the dog, wagging her tail at Bethany's feet.

A white snowshoe hare hopped along the edge of the spruce trees that bordered the back side of the ice rink, and Cupcake's ears pricked forward. The little dog kept her gaze glued to the bunny until it disappeared among the spindly, snow-covered evergreens, but didn't budge from her charge's side.

"We are," Bethany nodded.

They made their way back to the entrance of the rink, and Ella heard the racket taking place on the ice before she even opened the door. Inside, the sharp clacking of hockey sticks echoed off the high ceiling as Luke and Travis battled it out on the ice. Laughter mixed with the sound of their skate blades, but they weren't fooling anyone. They both had their eyes locked on to the puck that streaked over the ice, then bounced off the boards.

Travis lunged forward, shoulders low as he chased after it, but Luke was even quicker, his stick tapping against the puck with expert precision as he knocked it away with a controlled flick.

"That's all you got?" he taunted, breathless but grinning.

Her brother's only reply was a sharp cut to the right. There was a flash of movement, then the puck went flying toward the rickety goal they'd set up while Ella and Bethany had been outside.

They weren't just playing. They were treating this like it was some medieval joust—and here she was, the damsel in distress, apparently.

She almost snorted.

To them, she'd always be Travis's little sister, the girl who used to sit rinkside while they tore up the ice. They both still thought she was a kid who couldn't handle herself, like she needed her big brother or Luke—Luke, of all people—to fight her battles.

It infuriated her beyond belief.

"What are they doing?" Bethany asked, eyes huge in her face.

Ella rolled her eyes. *Acting like cavemen.* Or, more accurately, children. And they thought she was the one who wasn't a grown-up?

"They're playing hockey," she said flatly, signing the words in stilted movements that undoubtedly showcased her lack of enthusiasm for the juvenile display.

Someone was going to get hurt if they weren't careful, and Ella had zero intention of sticking around to play nursemaid to either of them.

"Ahem," she said loudly.

Out on the ice, Luke straightened and let the puck zip past him as he met her gaze. He offered her a sheepish, almost apologetic smile that tugged at her heartstrings despite her fierce determination to remain unfazed.

She wrapped her arms around her middle, holding herself together. There was nothing to apologize for. They'd nearly kissed, and then they hadn't. Ella preferred to think of it as divine intervention. God had just saved her from herself.

But after she left the rink, she headed directly to Helping Hounds, slammed her car into Park, and strode past Molly's desk without a word. Then she bypassed the hallway that led to her office and went straight to the kennel area for the dogs in the advanced service-dog program.

She could already hear Snickers's thick tail whacking into the sides of his kennel, as if he knew all along she'd come looking for him. Eventually, once she'd finally decided to choose him, just as he'd chosen her.

Ella had let her heart crack open today. At long last, she'd let down her guard, and there was no putting it back in place. She wished she could. Because now she was just as hurt and humiliated as she'd been the first time she'd thought Luke was the one. Maybe even more so, because now she knew something that she hadn't fully gasped until the moment Luke had skated away from her earlier.

Molly had been right all along: insisting on doing everything all on her own didn't make Ella a grown-up. It had simply made her lonely.

She opened the kennel door, bracing for Snickers's usual effusive greeting. The chocolate Lab didn't plow into her like he usually did, though. He hung his head low as he stepped slowly out of the kennel, then nudged his muzzle under her arm until he was situated flush against her side. The dog leaned into her with his full body weight, like he knew what she needed most in that moment was to feel his presence. Faithful. Steady. True.

His warm, solid form pressed into her, grounding her and reminding her that she wasn't alone. She never had been. It just felt that way sometimes.

"Thank You, God," she whispered and wiped a tear from her cheek with the back of her hand. "I guess I have a dog now."

This is enough, she told herself. She didn't need Luke Tanner—not then, and not anymore.

But when she wrapped her arms around Snickers and cried into his soft fur, the tears fell faster than he could lick them away.

Chapter Eleven

On Sunday, Luke and Bethany accompanied Gran to church at the white chapel that had stood in the heart of downtown Snowhaven since the Gold Rush.

It had been a while since Luke had been to a church service—longer than he cared to admit. In fact, the last time he'd attended worship had been in the same chapel when he'd been a teenager. Back then, he'd been a guest of the Grace family for Christmas Eve service his senior year. Now, he rode alongside a dozen or so senior citizens in the bus that Gran's assisted-living community used to shuttle residents to and fro.

"Doesn't it just look beautiful in the winter?" Gran said, breath fogging the vehicle's window as she pointed out the building with the tall, slender steeple to Bethany. "The chapel has always been the centerpiece of downtown, but I think it looks loveliest this time of year."

Gran was right. The crisp, white clapboards of the small-town church blended with the glittering snowy landscape and looked almost like something out of a storybook. Bethany clearly agreed, because she had stars in her eyes as they approached the parking lot.

"Thanks for inviting us to come with you, Gran," Luke said. "I hope you don't mind that we brought the dog. I called the church office to ask if emotional-support dogs were welcome, and they were very accommodating."

"Of course, I don't mind. And I'm not surprised a bit. The church is quite familiar with Helping Hounds. A few times a year, they even bring young puppies to Sunday services to help the dogs with their socialization." Gran chuckled. "Between you and me, I think the church is more than willing to help out. Attendance always goes up on those days. It's like Christmas and Easter rolled into one."

Luke laughed under his breath, despite the way his stomach twisted with unease as the bus lurched to a stop.

He'd figured he might run into Ella this morning, but if Helping Hounds had such a close relationship with the church, her presence at the service was all but certain. A few days ago, the possibility of seeing Ella would've been a welcome bonus. Now, Luke wasn't sure what to think.

She'd left the rink in a rush the other day after his hockey scrimmage with Travis. Luke had barely stepped off the ice before she headed for the door, and he'd had to stop himself from chasing after her. Her brother stayed for hours after she'd left, pitching in to help with some of the work around the shabby building. Together, they'd installed all the new Plexiglas shields at the top of the boards. Afterward, while Travis took over painting the trim, Luke repaired the holes in the nylon netting of the goal posts. He still wasn't convinced enough kids to start a junior hockey league would flock to the rink once it opened, but it wouldn't hurt to be ready, just in case.

He and Travis hadn't talked any more about Ella. In truth, they hadn't talked much about anything at all. Travis had always been more quiet than chatty. But Luke had been grateful for the help—even more so for the companionship. He'd invited Travis to go home with him and Bethany and order a pizza at dinnertime, but his friend had begged off. Still, the next afternoon he'd shown up back at the rink after leading a morning mushing excursion for a group of winter tourists, ready to help Luke with whatever else needed to be done.

It felt good to have a friend again, but Luke couldn't stop thinking about Ella. About that almost kiss...

"I'm going to help the bus driver get the passengers unloaded," he told Gran and Bethany, rising from his seat and hustling down the center aisle of the vehicle.

Most of the residents were fairly mobile, but a few used walkers and one of Gran's friends had rolled up to the bus in a motorized wheelchair, which was now stored in the cargo hold. Fortunately, the footpath leading up to the chapel had been freshly shoveled, so walking to the entrance wouldn't be too hazardous.

Luke hauled the wheelchair out of the back and, once it was in place, he offered his hand to help the elderly passengers as they made their way down the steps of the bus. The white shuttle sat humming at the curb, its wide doors and side-mounted wheelchair lift hinting at its purpose, while large block letters along the side spelled out *Snowhaven Assisted Living.* Luke liked being useful, and keeping busy might distract him from constantly looking for Ella.

He'd given it a lot of thought over the past couple days, and as right as that near kiss had felt, it would've been a mistake—and not just because she was Travis's little sister. Luke was in over his head enough already with Bethany. He didn't trust himself not to screw that up, and adding a romance with Ella to the mix would only make things ten times more dangerous.

He'd already messed up by pulling away from her when Travis had shown up so unexpectedly. Luke wasn't a complete knucklehead. He'd seen the hurt in her eyes afterward, and he'd been kicking himself ever since. That entire episode had reinforced what he already knew: he wasn't good enough for Ella.

He hadn't been deserving of the intense feelings she'd had for him back when they'd been kids. Anyone in Snowhaven would've agreed. What made him think this time was any different? While he'd been playing hockey for a living, she'd stayed right here and done something meaningful with her life.

Plus, she was an important part of Bethany's life. He had to think about more than just himself now. If he hurt Ella again, it could have devastating consequences for his niece. Bethany *needed* her.

Forgetting about what nearly happened between him and Ella was the right thing to do. The responsible thing.

"Thank you. You're such a dear," one of the senior ladies said as she descended the steps of the bus, squeezing his gloved hand tight.

"Happy to help." Luke offered her a polite smile, but his thoughts drifted back to skating with Ella and their near-kiss.

He shouldn't be thinking about her that way. Not now, and not here. But as the bus pulled away, Luke's gaze snagged on Ella standing beside her mother and Travis just outside the chapel's wooden double doors. Soft, golden light spilled from inside the church and surrounded her cinnamon hair like a halo. The sight of her, so effortlessly lovely, made one thing crystal clear—no matter how many times he tried to tamp it down, their brief moment of intimacy on the ice and the way she'd looked at him when they'd spun together wasn't something he could just forget.

However hard he tried.

"Oh, look. Luke's here." Ella's mom sat up straighter in the pew beside her and waved until Luke caught her eye from across the crowded chapel.

He waved back at Mom, and then his gaze shifted toward Ella. Her heart twisted as she looked away, focusing intently on the open hymnal in her lap until the black ink blurred before her eyes. She couldn't avoid him forever, obviously—not in a town this small and not when she'd had the brilliant idea to get his niece an emotional-support dog—but that didn't mean she was ready to face him quite yet.

His presence here had caught her off guard. She hadn't expected to see him walk through those chapel doors. Luke had never gone to church much when he was growing up.

"That must be his niece sitting beside him," Mom said, oblivious to the awkwardness weighing down on Ella's chest. "Is that the dog you helped them find, Ella?"

Ella forced herself to look, heart squeezing at the sight of Bethany with the deaf Cavalier curled on her lap. No matter what happened between her and Luke, she couldn't bring herself to regret matching Bethany with Cupcake.

What are you even talking about? Nothing *is happening between you and Luke.*

Right.

She swallowed hard. "Yes, that's Cupcake. Luke must've checked with the church to see if they could bring her."

Ugh, just when she'd managed to convince herself the

man had zero redeeming qualities, he went and proved her wrong. He'd made sure Bethany could bring her ESA to church, and there he was, sitting with his grandmother and a bunch of retirees. If that didn't cause a girl's heart to thaw, nothing would.

Not that she'd ever had any real trouble seeing Luke's good side. Pretending not to have feelings for him simply would've been easier if he didn't keep showing up and proving he wasn't the same reckless boy she used to know.

She took a deep breath and started counting the seconds until the service started. The sooner it did, the sooner it would be over with and she could get out of here and breathe again.

"You okay, sis?" Travis asked, poking her in the ribs with his elbow. "You seem a little tense."

Ella forced a smile and shook her head. "I'm fine."

Travis tilted his head, regarding her and Luke in turn as his gaze flitted back and forth between them. "You sure about that?"

How much had he seen the other day when he'd burst into the rink? Ella hadn't asked, and other than his weird game of one-on-one hockey with Luke, Travis hadn't offered up any commentary. She sent up a silent prayer it stayed that way.

"I told you I'm fine," she whispered through gritted teeth. Maybe she should tell him she'd officially adopted Snickers. That was a surefire way to change the subject, although she wasn't exactly in the mood for a brotherly I-told-you-so.

"You do seem a little wound up, honey," Mom said on the other side of her. Then she took Ella's hand and pressed something inside it. "Maybe this will help cheer you up."

She gasped as her fingers closed around the smooth, familiar shape of another wood carving.

Her breath caught as she turned it over in her palm, tracing the delicate details with her fingertips. This one was a mama bear with two baby cubs peeking out from beneath her two front legs. The texture of the mother bear's thick fur was carved into the soft silver spruce in pricked, careful strokes. She was a grizzly. The curves of her massive shoulders contrasted with the fine, almost fragile intricacy of the cubs nestled protectively in her shadow. Their tiny paws and wide, trusting eyes had been perfectly captured in the grain.

"It's us," she said in an awestruck whisper. "You, me, and Travis."

She turned to show the carving to her brother, but he just shrugged. "Yeah, she showed it to me earlier."

Could he be less interested? Ella would never understand men—another perfectly valid reason why Snickers should be the only one in her life.

She turned to search their mother's face. Mom's eyes glittered in the gentle gold light of the chapel.

"Another holy whisper," she said with a slight hitch in her breath. "I have to say, this one is my favorite so far."

Of course, it was. The carving was tailor-made for her, a celebration of motherhood, just like the wooden dog left behind at Helping Hounds had been especially meaningful to Ella. Whoever was whittling these figures wasn't only familiar with Dad's art, but they also knew a fair bit about Ella's family. Who could it possibly be?

"Where did this come from?" she pressed. "When did you find it?"

"Shh." Travis nudged her again with his elbow and tipped his head toward the altar. The choir had begun to sing, their voices lifting in harmony. "The service is starting."

He rose to his feet, and Mom did, too.

Ella reluctantly followed suit. As the service went on, her mind struggled to stay focused on the hymns and the pastor's sermon. The minutes seemed to stretch out, and the warmth of the chapel began to feel stifling as snow tapped softly against the windows. When she wasn't thinking about the mysterious carvings, she found herself sneaking glances at Luke sitting quietly on the opposite side of the aisle. His expression was unreadable, even when he occasionally glanced up and caught her looking. By the time the pastor recited the final blessing, Ella was restless, eager to escape the weight of the moment.

"I need some fresh air. I'll meet you and Trav outside," she said, giving her mother a quick kiss on the cheek as the parishioners began to stand up and exchange pleasantries.

Ella moved quickly, her chest tightening with a dozen different emotions she couldn't quite identify as she headed toward the door, weaving deftly between churchgoers lingering in the aisle.

Just as she spilled out onto the chapel's wide front porch, Luke's voice stopped her in her tracks.

"Ella."

Just her name—that's all he said, but somehow it was still enough to make her heart tumble.

She turned around. "Hey."

"Hey." He lifted a single eyebrow. "Are you running from me, Elly Bean?"

"No," she said quickly. A little *too* quickly, actually.

He studied her for a long moment, until her face went

warm in the frigid air. "We're okay, aren't we? About the other day…"

She shook her head. She couldn't talk about this right now—not at church, of all places. "Everything is fine, I promise. We just got caught up in the moment, that's all."

His eyes narrowed, probably because she'd injected her voice with so much false cheer that she sounded like she might be trying to convince herself more than him.

"Caught up in the moment," he echoed. Two lines formed between his eyebrows, and Ella couldn't tell if the quiet pull of his words meant he was disappointed or relieved.

"Yep, that's all." She'd rather die on the spot than have him think she was secretly in love with him—*again*—even though she wasn't altogether sure it wasn't true. "You don't have to worry. It won't happen again."

"Good," he said, and the lines between his eyebrows etched even deeper, like he was agreeing to something he didn't quite believe. "I'm glad we're on the same page."

Then why did he look like he'd just swallowed a mouthful of glass?

Ella gripped the sleeves of her coat, fingers curling around the crimson wool. She waited for relief to set in. After all, this was what she'd wanted—to smooth things over and go back to how things had been before a silly moment of weakness unraveled everything between them. But Luke's tortured expression made that impossible.

Part of her wanted to press and force him to admit he wasn't telling the whole truth. He'd felt something when they'd almost kissed. They both had.

But the other part of her, the part that remembered what it felt like to love someone who didn't love her back, just couldn't do it.

"Tomorrow's the big day, right?" she said in an effort to switch conversational gears.

Luke nodded. "Yep, first day of school."

"I'll see you and Bethany in the morning." Ella would never bail on Luke's niece, no matter how uncomfortable she felt around him at the moment. "Cupcake, too, obviously."

He offered her a half grin. "Obviously."

The chapel doors swished open and the other parishioners began filtering out of the chapel, swallowing her and Luke up in a flurry of happy conversation. Ella needed to get out of there pronto. Her cheeks were beginning to hurt from the effort it took to keep smiling.

"'Bye, Luke," she said, and then she turned to go before he could respond so she didn't do something dumb, like look back.

She felt his gaze on her back the entire time, nonetheless, warming her from the inside out like a luminous midnight sun.

Chapter Twelve

Luke kept as busy as possible for the rest of the day. If he remained still for longer than a minute or two, his thoughts inevitably began to ping-pong from one anxiety to the next. Despite every effort not to dwell on Bethany's first day of school, a countdown was already playing itself out in his head, ticking relentlessly toward the moment he'd have to leave her there all by herself. Whenever he managed to push aside that internal clock, snatches of his conversation with Ella at church came rushing back, which only made him feel worse.

Were they really on the same page? He wished he knew. Then again, if Ella truly didn't have feelings for him, maybe he was better off in the dark.

Once the bus carted them back to the assisted-living facility after church, Luke and Bethany spent most of the afternoon with Gran. Travis did handiwork around Gran's room, like changing light bulbs, tightening loose door handles, and replacing the batteries in the TV remote and the cuckoo clock Gramps had gotten her years ago when he'd been stationed at an army base in Germany. Bethany had been wanting Gran to teach her how to crochet, so he'd stopped by the yarn store a few days ago and picked up a ball of pink yarn and a large-gauged hook that the woman at the counter had told him was best for children. He'd saved them as a surprise, hoping a new craft project would help keep any school jitters at bay on the last day of winter break.

"These are for me?" Bethany asked when he handed her the bundle of yarn, speared through with the crochet hook, her voice a mixture of astonishment and anticipation.

"I thought now might be a good time to give it a try." Luke winked and gave her a reassuring nod. The way he saw it, he might not be the only one who needed a distraction today. "There's no one better than Gran to show you how. She's got all sorts of tricks up her sleeve."

"That's right." The older woman nodded as she moved from her favorite recliner to the small sofa situated along the adjacent wall. She patted the empty space beside her and crooked a finger at Bethany. "Come here, dear. I'll get you crocheting in no time."

A couple of hours later, Bethany had completed a collection of simple chain bracelets—a perfect beginner project for young children, according to Gran. They were stacked all up and down her slender arm, from wrist to .elbow. She'd struggled with the stitches at first, but caught on far quicker than Luke expected. He shouldn't have been so surprised—the precise finger movements and hand coordination required for sign language made her a natural at yarn art. By the time they packed up and headed home, Cupcake sported a pink crochet collar that matched Bethany's bracelets.

"Did you have a nice day?" Luke signed as he tucked his niece into bed later that night. She smelled like bubble bath and baby powder and a little bit like Cupcake's favorite hot-dog treats—scents of a happy, innocent girlhood that made Luke's chest tighten with something bittersweet.

She nodded, head snug against her pillow with her honey-blond hair fanned out around her angelic face. A sleepy smile tugged at the corners of her mouth, and Cupcake was already doing the slow-blink thing that puppies did when they were about to curl into sleep.

"You ready for tomorrow?" he signed, fingers moving slower this time. Hesitating ever so slightly.

Bethany gave a small head bob. "I think so."

Luke wished she sounded more confident, but who could blame her?

He pressed a kiss to her forehead and signed, "You're going to do amazing."

He hoped she didn't notice the slight tremor in his hands as they moved from a double high five into a double low five, the ASL sign for *amazing*. All day, he'd been running from his feelings, but they'd caught up to him all the same.

"Good night, kiddo," he murmured, signing the words at the same time.

"Good night, Uncle Luke," she signed back. Then her eyes drifted closed as he got up, flipped off the overhead light, and adjusted the door until it was halfway shut.

He paused in the hallway, listening as her breathing evened out. Then, with a quiet exhale, he snuck a final glance at the peaceful rise and fall of her tiny form under the blankets.

The floorboards in Gran's old Gold Rush cottage groaned under his feet as he made his way to his room. The heater kicked on with its usual tick-tick-tick, and he had a flashback to an overnight visit here when he'd been a kid. He must've been about Bethany's age, and while his parents had been away on a trip, he and Steven had stayed with Gran.

In a million years, he would've never guessed that he'd find his way back to this same house as an adult, kissing a little girl on her forehead and wishing her sweet dreams. This life was everything Luke had been trying to escape when he left town—not because he didn't want it, but because he'd never felt like *it* wanted *him*.

But by the grace of God, here he was.

They were going to make it here, weren't they? Things in Snowhaven hadn't been perfect so far, but Bethany was still okay. *They* were okay.

They just had to make it through tomorrow. Then the next day, and the one after that, and so on, and so on. At church this morning—when his gaze hadn't been drifting toward Ella—Luke had managed to catch snatches of the pastor's sermon. He'd talked about a verse from Matthew that encouraged believers to take things one day at a time.

Take therefore no thought for the morrow: for the morrow shall take thought for the things of itself. Sufficient unto the day is the evil thereof.

Luke squeezed his eyes closed.

I'm trying, God. I'm trying.

Later that night, after he'd shrugged out of his flannel and sunk into bed, he stared at the ceiling, unable to sleep. He needed rest in the worst way, and he told himself that sleep would come if he could just quiet his mind. Going over the list of things he needed to do at the rink while Bethany was at school wasn't helping, and neither was thinking about Ella. Her porcelain skin against the cherry-red coat with the silver fur collar she'd been wearing this morning… The way she'd kept seeking out his gaze during the service when she clearly didn't want to… The forced cheer in her voice when she'd told him not to worry.

It won't happen again.

A wistfulness wound its way through him as he turned onto his side and stared at the shadows stretching across the ceiling. He wasn't sure when he finally fell asleep, but at some point he must have, because hours later, he jerked awake to the sound of a scream.

His heart slammed against his rib cage as he sat up, blinking into the darkness.

Bethany?

Another scream came from the direction of her bedroom, followed by a loud sob. Luke threw off the covers and ran down the hall. No matter how many nightmares the child had, he'd never get used to them. Each one tore at his heart, just a little bit more than the last.

This one was the most devastating of all, though. Bethany hadn't had any nightmares since they'd adopted Cupcake. He'd foolishly thought they'd become a thing of the past, but no. She loved that dog with her whole heart, but stitching a broken little girl back together overnight was a task too big for anyone, least of all a six-month-old puppy.

"I'm here," he whispered into her hair as she sobbed into his shoulder. He knew she couldn't hear him, but he couldn't just stay silent. Doing so would only make the helpless feeling in the pit of his stomach worse. Besides, maybe she could feel the vibrations in his chest as he spoke, and that sensation would root her here in the present moment, where she was safe and sound. "It's okay, sweetheart. I'm here."

Cupcake tried to nudge her way in between Luke and Bethany, and at first, he held her back. The dog was relentless, though—whining and pawing at Luke's arm—until he finally relented. Then, goose bumps prickled over his skin as the little dog licked Bethany's hands, poked her muzzle into the child's side, and seemed to do everything within her power to drag Bethany out of her bad dream.

To his astonishment, it worked. Bethany hiccupped, her tears finally beginning to ebb. Cupcake burrowed into her lap, snuggling her head under Bethany's hand repeatedly until Luke's niece wiped at her face and began petting the dog. Before long, a whisper of a smile tugged at the corners of her mouth. Then she rested her head on her pillow again and curled into Cupcake's soft warmth, her eyelids growing heavy again.

The panic in Luke's gut finally began to uncoil, and a bone-deep relief took its place, but it was still a fragile thing. Still temporary. Still something he wasn't sure he could trust. A thin layer of ice over deep, black water.

Ella could tell right away that something was wrong when she and Snickers met Luke, Bethany, and Cupcake on the sidewalk in front of their cottage Monday morning.

Snowhaven Elementary was within easy walking distance from the downtown neighborhood where Ella's little rental home stood, a mere two blocks away from the house where Luke's grandmother had lived before she'd moved into her assisted-living community.

It was Luke's house now, Ella thought. Although, he looked anything but at home and comfortable as she and Snickers approached. Granted, he was a big, burly hockey player—a sharp contrast to the Queen Anne-style cottage that stood behind him, with its fanciful Victorian trim and pastel-colored shingles. Like the other homes in the area, it looked almost like a dollhouse. Wraparound porches and intricate gables were all the rage back in the late 1800s, when the Gold Rush changed the Alaskan landscape. Snowhaven was a living testament to that transformation—grace amid the wild, rugged beauty of the Alaskan frontier.

The house wasn't what made Luke look so out of sorts, though. The poor guy obviously hadn't slept much the night before. A stab of sympathy poked through her resistance as she took in the shadows under his eyes and the flat set of his mouth. She'd been determined to focus exclusively on Bethany and Cupcake this morning, with as little interaction with Luke as she could get away with.

So much for self-preservation.

"Good morning," she said, signing the greeting at the same time, lifting her hand to mimic the sun coming up. Her eyes flitted from Bethany to Luke, and her heart gave a traitorous flutter. "Everything okay?"

"Great." He nodded and offered her a thoroughly unconvincing smile. "Bethany's ready for her first day at Snowhaven Elementary, right, sweetheart?"

He placed his big palm in the center of the little girl's back, and she nodded. A mixture of excitement and worry glittered in her big blue eyes. Cupcake stayed glued right by her side, even as Snickers wagged his entire back end and greeted the little Cavalier with an enthusiastically clumsy touch of his big nose to her tiny, button one.

Something definitely felt off.

Ella squatted in front of Bethany so she could fully meet her gaze. "You're going to have so much fun today. Did Uncle Luke tell you that Snowhaven Elementary is where he and your daddy both went to school? And me, too."

Bethany looked up at her uncle for confirmation, and he nodded with a slightly more convincing grin.

"I like your bracelets," Ella said, running the pad of her thumb over the pink yarn. These were new, and they looked like something Luke's grandmother might've had a hand in. "Did you make them yourself?"

"They're friendship bracelets," Bethany nodded, then removed one of them from her arm, and offered it to Ella. "You can have one if you want."

"Thank you." Ella slipped the yarn over her hand, the carefully stitched loops stretching just enough to accommodate the size of an adult wrist. "Look how pretty!"

Bethany shifted from foot to foot and stood a little taller. "I made them for the new friends I'm going to make at school today. Do you think they'll like them?"

"I know they will." Ella reached out and tucked a golden lock behind her ear. Someone—Luke, she presumed—had woven Bethany's hair into double French braids. *Impressive.* Just another chink in her armor where a certain single dad was concerned. "Shall we get on our way? You don't want to be late."

Bethany made a knocking motion with her fist. *Yes.*

They walked the short distance to the school, led by Snickers and Cupcake, who wagged their tails in unison like two mismatched sled dogs at the head of a sled. Walking had been a good call on Luke's part, despite the cold. It gave everyone a few minutes to shake off their nerves. By the time they arrived at the steps leading up to the building, Bethany appeared far more relaxed—excited, even. Especially when her teacher, Miss Carmichael, met them just outside the school's entrance.

She greeted Bethany in ASL and then petted both dogs, a sure sign to Ella that Bethany was in good hands.

"She's going to be fine, Luke," Ella said with a gentle

nudge after she'd disappeared inside the building with her hand tucked into Miss Carmichael's.

He nodded at the same time his forehead creased in confusion. "I didn't realize those were friendship bracelets."

"She's excited about making friends, even after the bullying she experienced at her old school. I think that's a good sign." Ella reached out and squeezed his hand before she could think better of it.

He squeezed it back, so tightly that a pulse of warmth shot through her. She did not have feelings for him, she reminded herself. She was just being his friend.

And he sure seemed to need one at that moment.

"She had another nightmare last night," he said quietly, then swallowed so hard that Ella could hear the movement of his throat, like a stone had lodged there. "A bad one."

"I'm sure that was hard," Ella said.

"Cupcake helped, though. It was kinda special to see." He glanced down at the dog, and his expression softened as he recounted the events of the night before to Ella.

When he finished, she bent down to tell the Cavalier she was a good girl. Not one to be ignored, Snickers poked his cold nose against her cheek and nearly knocked her over.

Luke laughed at the Lab's antics, and Ella was so glad to see him relax a bit that she'd have gladly let the goofy dog knock her over if necessary.

Luke helped her up before he had a chance. "Are you absolutely sure that dog is cut out to be a service animal? I know you're the expert, not me, but I've got some doubts."

She shook her head and took a deep breath. "Actually, I've decided to adopt him myself. It just feels right."

"I think that's a good call. He's clearly head over heels for you."

At least someone is.

Ella felt her smile go a bit wobbly, so she steered things back to safer territory. "I'm sorry Bethany had another nightmare, but I'm glad Cupcake did her job last night. She's as devoted to your niece as Snickers is to me."

Luke tugged at the edges of his knit beanie, pushing it back slightly on his head. "I just kind of thought those days were behind us, you know. It made me wonder if Bethany is truly ready for today."

"She's ready. Those bracelets don't lie." Ella offered him an encouraging smile, but she knew already that she couldn't just leave him alone with his thoughts for the rest of the day. He needed a distraction, and she knew the perfect one. "Having an emotional-support dog isn't a quick fix. Healing takes time, even when you have help. Bethany might still have bad days, but she'll also have good ones. More good ones than you'll ever be able to count. I can prove it to you."

He gave her a sideways glance. "How?"

"You'll see." She tugged him away from the school by the elbow of his parka. "Come with me."

Chapter Thirteen

Luke spent the rest of the school day at Helping Hounds, mostly because Ella simply wouldn't take no for an answer.

Admittedly, he didn't put up much of a fight. Since Travis had been pitching in so much at the ice rink, the place was already looking halfway decent—as good as could be expected, given Luke's limited budget for repairs and improvements. Barring any disasters, things were mostly on track for the grand reopening party this coming Saturday.

Mainly, though, he didn't want to be alone—not today. He knew he could've spent the day with Gran. Travis might've even let him tag along on a mushing excursion. But no one could get him out of his head like Ella could, so when she walked him to her house and ordered him to get inside the car and accompany her to work, he did as she said.

Ella drove a sport utility vehicle, which seemed like it had been designed for two purposes: navigating the extreme Alaskan winters and transporting dogs. A net barrier separated the front seat from the back seat. Snickers and Cupcake sat side by side with their noses poked through the mesh holes like two canine clowns, and Luke realized this excursion was probably the best thing he could've done for Bethany's dog. Cupcake had whined for a few minutes and paced at the end of her leash after Bethany disappeared inside the school. Luke hadn't been prepared to deal with the dog's emotions on top of his own, but she seemed to like hanging out with Snickers. Who wouldn't? The chocolate Lab was joy on four paws.

"Okay, boss," Luke said, rolling up the sleeves of his flannel overshirt after they'd stowed their coats in her office and she'd led him to the kennel area. "What do you want me to do?"

She handed him a stainless steel scoop and pointed at the neatly organized rows of large plastic bins full of kibble. "For starters, why don't you prepare breakfast for everyone? That's the fastest way to make friends around here."

She winked at him, and for a second, he wondered if she'd just tricked him into providing her company with a day's worth of free labor as payback for the botched kiss. What could feeding a bunch of service dogs in training teach him about healing?

Luke knew Ella better than that, though. And she knew dogs like no one else he'd ever encountered. If she thought there was something he could learn from them here today, then he was all in.

So he did as she asked and worked his way down the line of kennels, filling one bowl after another. The dogs bounced with anticipation. Cupcake gobbled up the few stray pieces of kibble he dropped, chasing them as they skittered across the tile floor. In under an hour, everyone had full bellies and the set of Luke's shoulders had indeed relaxed somewhat.

That was only the beginning, though. Next, Ella blindfolded him and had him role-play as a handler for some of the future guide dogs in the advanced training class. He practiced basic obedience with some of the younger dogs. Then, as the clock crept closer to school-dismissal time, he sat in on a session where a handler and a service dog were paired together for the very first time. The emotional moment hit Luke harder than he'd expected.

Afterward, when he took a few of the dogs into the exercise area behind the main building, a golden retriever with a coat as glossy and red as a copper penny rested its chin on his knee as he sat and watched from a bench in the fenced-in yard. The pup looked at him with soulful eyes, as if it could see straight through to the guarded parts of himself that Luke wasn't ready to unpack. He hesitated and then buried his fingers in the dog's thick fur, surprisingly warm in the chill of the outdoor air. The other dogs raced around the yard, tumbling after one another, but this one stayed put, content to just sit with him—a quiet companion with no judgment and no expectations. Only a steady, calming presence. Before Luke realized what was happening, he got misty-eyed.

Maybe there really was something to this whole healing thing, after all.

"That's Grady," Ella said softly from behind him, her voice gentle with understanding. "He's a special boy, and he's going to make a great service dog someday for a veteran with PTSD."

He'd been so transfixed by the golden that he hadn't heard her enter the exercise pen.

"I believe it," Luke said, fingertips burrowing deeper into the dog's coat. "I didn't realize dogs could help with things like that."

Ella sat down beside him and rubbed her mittened

hands together. "They sure can. I think it's because dogs just understand, you know."

"Understand what, exactly?" he asked, finally breaking the sweet dog's gaze to look at her.

Wow, she was beautiful. The realization shouldn't have caught him by surprise the way it did. He'd spent plenty of time with her since moving back to Snowhaven, and when he closed his eyes at night, her heart-shaped face and kind eyes floated around in his mind's eye. But seeing her here, working with the dogs all day…it was different. Special. She *glowed*. Here, she was in her element, and it showed.

"They understand living in the moment in a way that humans never will. We get so caught up in the past, but they don't. People hang on to everything. Even when the bad times are behind us, we still carry the hurt around. Try as we might, sometimes we get so caught up in that pain that we convince ourselves the good times might never come—not because there's nothing good left in the world, but because we don't deserve it." Her eyes went shiny, and then a pink flush settled in her cheeks.

He hoped she wasn't talking about herself because if anyone deserved everything good that life had to offer, it was Ella.

He also knew that if she was carrying around any past hurts, he'd been the cause of at least some of them.

"It's just a theory I have." She let out a slow, foggy exhale and looked away, focusing on the dogs romping and playing in the exercise yard instead of him.

Grady lifted his chin from Luke's knee and trotted off to join the party, and he couldn't help but wonder if the gentle dog sensed how badly Luke wanted a moment alone with her.

"So according to this theory, we should all be more like dogs." Luke bit back a smile. "Guess this means I don't stand a chance against Snickers."

He snuck a sidelong look at her just in time to see the corner of her bow-shaped lips twitch, like she was fighting back a grin. He knew he shouldn't be flirting with her, but he couldn't help it. Neither one of them had been completely honest at church yesterday. Luke knew it as surely as he knew Ella was a dog person as opposed to a cat person.

"Snickers is pretty perfect," she said without meeting his gaze, but he could hear the humor in her voice.

So are you.

He pushed that thought away before it could take root. He was already skating on dangerously thin ice, talking to her like this. It was so easy to with Ella, though—too easy. If he wasn't careful, he might make a habit out of it.

We just got caught up in the moment.

That's how she'd explained away their near kiss. Luke had turned those words over in his head time and time again, and right now, he had to bite his tongue from asking her if she wanted to get caught up in another moment. Maybe even *this* moment.

Her eyes slid toward him, and her forehead scrunched when she took in his expression. "What? Why are you looking at me like that?"

Luke shrugged. "Snickers is great, but he's far from perfect."

They were, after all, talking about a large dog that liked to nap in the middle of her desk. Also, he had to say something, and telling her he was thinking about kissing her was decidedly off the table.

She gave him a lighthearted shoulder bump. "Don't

insult the love of my life like that. I adore him uncondi-
tionally."

Luke nodded resolutely. "As you should."

She grinned, and their gazes caught for a second or
two. Those five words hovered between them, though,
pulsing with meaning. *The love of my life.* Tiny gold flecks
glittered in the depths of her soft brown irises—hidden
treasure, just like the gold that had lured so many others
to this place hundreds of years ago.

She cleared her throat and looked away. "It's about
time for school to get out. I know you're probably anxious
to get over there and see how Bethany's first day went."

He was. But he also wished they could sit together for
the rest of the day, talking until the sun went down. The
hope stirring in his chest was nothing but fool's gold,
though.

They were friends. Period.

"You're right." Luke's gaze fell to the ground, where a
flurry of paw prints circled his boots in the snow. She'd
let him in today—into her world and into her trust. He
wasn't about to do anything to mess that up again. "Let's
go, Elly Bean."

They stopped for coffee on the way, and Ella gave Luke
a thorough education on pup cups—the small paper cups
of whipped topping that most coffee shops offered for
free to their canine patrons. So it was really no surprise
that Snickers and Cupcake both sported whipped cream
mustaches as the four of them stood outside the elementary school, waiting for Bethany.

Ella sipped her mocha and tried not to think about how
nice it would be to do this on a regular basis. Today had
been a novelty, that's all. Surely this warm, fuzzy family

feeling that had wrapped itself around her like a blanket would get old after a while.

Sure. Keep telling yourself that.

She buried her face into her take-out cup in case Luke was able to take one glance at her and read her mind. She knew he couldn't, but he had a way of looking at her sometimes that made her feel as transparent as frost on a windowpane.

"Get the hot cocoa ready," she said as she glanced up and spotted Bethany's blond braids in the crowd of kids who burst from the door mere seconds after the bell rang. "Here she comes."

Luke gripped the hot chocolate he'd gotten her at the coffee shop as he searched the group of children for a glimpse of his niece. His knuckles looked like they were on the verge of turning white.

"If you squeeze that paper cup any harder, you're going to end up with cocoa all over yourself, Dad," Ella teased.

He laughed under his breath as he readjusted his grip on the cup, and then he blinked at her. "Did you just call me 'Dad'?"

"Um, yes." Had that been the wrong thing to say? She didn't mean to disrespect Steven's memory, but Luke was giving off some serious dad energy right now.

She wished she could say it wasn't the least bit endearing, but tragically, that would've been a lie bigger than Alaska—which happened to be *double* the size of Texas.

Ella gnawed on her bottom lip. "Is that okay?"

"I'm not sure. I guess so—it just caught me off guard." His brow furrowed. "The adoption paperwork has already been filed with the courts. I'm just waiting on our copies of the final order from the judge in Oregon. Even then,

I'll just always think of Steven as Bethany's dad. I'm sure everyone will."

"You know what I think?" She gave him a gentle hip check. "I think you mean more to Bethany than you realize."

The frown lines around his mouth deepened. "I've never really been father material. You know that as well as anyone."

Did he genuinely not realize how much that little girl loved him?

"Now, you listen to me, Luke Tanner. You are—" Ella froze before she could tell him that he was one-thousand-percent father material. It was her turn to blink now because she was pretty convinced she was hallucinating.

"Uncle Luke!" Bethany threw herself into Luke's arms with a grin on her face that spread from ear to ear. Ella did her best to take in the heartwarming scene, but she couldn't focus on anything but the little girl's hand...

And the small wooden carving that was clutched tightly in her fingers.

"Hey there, kiddo," Luke said, pulling back just enough for Bethany to read his lips. "It seems like you had a pretty good first day at your new school."

"The best day." Bethany dropped to her knees to greet Cupcake, and the glitter on her bubblegum-hued backpack glimmered in the sunshine. "I made some new friends."

Two girls who looked like they were about the same age caught Bethany's gaze as they walked past and waved. Friendship bracelets made of pink yarn dangled from both of their slim wrists. "'Bye, Bethany!"

Bethany waved back. "'Bye, Lila. 'Bye, Wren."

"Go ahead, Elly Bean," Luke murmured under his breath. "Say 'I told you so.' I know you want to."

He chuckled, but as soon as he tore his gaze away from Bethany to regard Ella, his tone changed abruptly. "Ella? What's wrong? You look like you just saw a ghost."

She released a tremulous exhale. That's precisely what she felt like every time another animal carving appeared—like she'd just seen her father's ghost. It wasn't true, obviously. But every time a new one popped up, a wave of goose bumps washed over her, from the top of her head to the tips of her toes.

"I'm fine. It's just…" She drew in a slow breath. Where to start?

Ella hadn't told Luke about the new animal carvings. He was one of the few people in Snowhaven who'd known about her dad's whittling, though. He'd spent enough time at their house as a kid to have seen Dad in action, pocket-knife in hand. When he and Travis got stir-crazy inside the log house or started waving their hockey sticks around indoors, Dad would sometimes send them outside to hunt for usable chunks of spruce.

"What is it?" Luke asked, and then his eyes traced the path of her stare. "Whoa. Is that…?"

Bethany straightened and held out the figurine. "Look what I found inside my cubby today. Miss Carmichael said I could keep it."

Ella's gaze bore into the small wooden figure. Like the others, it had been carved in a style similar to her father's, from the same familiar-looking wood. This one was a young reindeer with small buds of brand-new antlers on its head. The animal had long, fluttery eyelashes, and since both male and female caribou grew antlers, Ella just knew it was meant to be a girl reindeer. The bow carved just above the caribou's left ear eliminated any and all doubts.

It's Bethany. She swallowed. *Just like the mama bear*

*and the two cubs were supposed to be Mom, Travis,
and me.*

The carvings were getting more personal, and they
weren't popping up in random public places anymore.
These weren't supposed to be surprise gifts to the community like the ones her dad had done. Every carving that
had appeared since the moose had been tailor-made to
be found by someone. The dog, bears, and reindeer were
all bespoke gifts made with a specific recipient in mind.
First her, then Mom, and now Bethany.

Luke's gaze softened as he studied the figurine. "It's
a little reindeer. Bethany, sweetheart, someone left this
in your cubby?"

She nodded. "It was there this morning when Miss
Carmichael showed me where to put my things. She said
maybe you left it there for me as a surprise for my first
day."

"It wasn't me." He shook his head and glanced at Ella.
"Isn't this one of your dad's? Did you...?"

She held up her hands. "Not me. And not Dad, either,
I'm afraid."

He focused on the caribou carving again, forehead
crinkling. "I don't understand. It looks just like the ones
he used to make when we were kids. You've got a whole
shelf of them in your office."

"I can explain." Could she, though? She was no closer
to solving this mystery than when she first began. Ella
should've paid more attention to all those TV mystery
shows she loved so much. A detective, she was not.

She sighed. "Sort of."

Chapter Fourteen

In the week leading up to the grand reopening of the ice skating rink, the carved animal pieces stopped appearing. Ella could only assume that she was either looking in the wrong places, or the mystery whittler had decided to take a break. Or perhaps the old adage that a watched pot never boils was at play because ever since the reindeer with the bow by her ear had turned up in Bethany's cubby at school, Ella had indeed been on the lookout.

She kept her eyes peeled everywhere she went. Now that she'd told Luke the whole story about the carvings, he'd also been on the hunt for any clues about the artist's identity. Even Snickers was on high alert, likely picking up on Ella's energy. Whenever they were out and about, his brown head swiveled back and forth and he sniffed the air like a search dog. Ella just wasn't altogether sure the goofball knew what he was searching for.

Unfortunately, since the animal figures had stopped popping up, the investigation had gotten exactly nowhere. Which was probably for the best, considering how busy everyone had been getting ready for Luke's big celebration.

"I can't believe today's the day," Molly said as she

helped Ella load a group of the guide and service-dog trainees into the back of her SUV on Saturday morning.

When Ella had offered to bring a few dogs to the party at the rink, Luke had loved the idea. Helping Hounds trainees were always a big hit when they were out in the community. The more, the merrier. She'd had to put her foot down, though, when Travis suggested outfitting the dogs in hockey gear.

Ella buckled a black Lab named Midnight into a seat harness and shut the back door of the vehicle. Everyone was locked and loaded. She grinned at Molly. "I can't believe it, either. This week has been a whirlwind."

She'd been at the rink almost every night this week, working alongside Travis and Luke. At first, it felt a little odd. Every time Ella and Luke shared a laugh or a stolen moment, she felt Travis's eyes on them. But after a day or two, things fell into a comfortable and familiar rhythm. It was almost like old times.

Maybe a little too much *like old times*, Ella thought, since a warm thrill skipped through her chest whenever she was around Luke. Her schoolgirl crush was alive and well. She was trying to keep it in check, but spending so much time with him was beginning to be a problem— a problem she seemed to have no intention of fixing at the moment.

She'd deal with it later, after the grand reopening. That's what she told herself, anyway, as she climbed behind the wheel and Molly took her place in the passenger seat. Ella would act as Snickers's handler at the party, Molly had volunteered to be on the other end of Midnight's leash, and a few of the Helping Hounds volunteer puppy raisers were scheduled to meet them at the rink to work with the other dogs. Ella had also contacted a few local reporters that Willow had worked with in the past to help promote Helping Hounds, and two of them had agreed to attend the event and cover the ice rink's reopening for the local paper and television station. Everything was falling neatly into place.

"Wow, I can't believe how great it looks in here," Molly said after they'd gotten the dogs unloaded and led them into the rink, all decked out in their Helping Hounds working-dog vests.

"It's kind of unbelievable, isn't it? The rink has never looked so good." Ella's chest swelled with pride as she looked around. It wasn't just that the old building had gotten a good scrubbing and a fresh coat of paint. Luke and Travis had stayed up half the night inflating hundreds of helium balloons that now hung from the ceiling in the lobby. Colorful streamers stretched over the ice, and a giant red, white, and blue balloon arch flanked the entrance. Hockey-themed garlands covered the concession area, with illustrated pucks, hockey skates, and crisscrossed hockey sticks decorating the paper flags. Luke had even managed to get the vintage popcorn machine back in working order, and the scent of buttery fresh popcorn hung heavy in the air.

Go big, or go home. That had been the mantra Luke and Travis had been repeating all week, punctuated with occasional high fives. Bethany had even gotten in on the action, jumping up to slap their palms while Cupcake reared up her hind legs, eager to join in. Now that everything was in full swing, Ella doubted anyone in the entire state of Alaska would argue that Luke hadn't poured his heart and soul into this project.

"He's already had a dozen kids sign interest forms for a new junior hockey league," Travis said as he grinned at Ella and welcomed Snickers with a scratch behind his ears. "The Ice Crushers live on."

"He's seriously going with that name?" Ella laughed.

"You bet. I'm just not sure what he's going to call the other team if he gets enough kids for two separate squads."

Ella opened her mouth to make the obvious suggestion, but Travis held up a hand before she could get it out.

"Do not say the Rink Rats." He shot her a mock glare.

That's exactly what she'd intended on saying. "Okay, I won't, but you know I was thinking it."

"Well, how does it look?" Luke darted over to them and greeted Ella with a peck on the cheek.

His hand was warm on the center of her back, and she had to stop herself from turning her head a few degrees so the kiss landed on her lips. *Nope, not going there.* She took a deep inhale. The chill wafting toward her from the ice was clearly messing with her head.

"It looks incredible, Luke. You must be so proud," she said. He hadn't mentioned his money troubles since the first few times they'd talked about it, but the turnout was great, and the party had just gotten started. Surely with the rink open for public skating and the potential for a youth hockey program, he'd be able to turn things around. *Please, God.*

"I think Gran is proud enough for the both of us," Luke said, and a sheepish grin creased his face as he nodded toward the concession area, where his grandmother stood surrounded by a group of friends from her retirement community. "It looks like she recruited half the residents of Snowhaven Assisted Living into baking treats. She's even got Bethany passing out cookies."

Ella waved at Luke's niece, beaming in a retro-style apron that had probably come straight from Gran's kitchen. She held a tray piled high with cookies, and as usual, Cupcake was glued to her side. Ella knew they needed to keep a close eye on the Cavalier today. Deaf dogs weren't as affected by the noise and commotion of large crowds as hearing dogs were, but she didn't want Bethany's pup to get startled by sudden movements or unexpected touches. So far, so good, though. Cupcake appeared to be handling the gathering just as Ella expected—by relying on visual cues from Bethany. Her big brown eyes rarely strayed from the little girl.

Luke leaned toward Ella and whispered into her ear. "Some of Bethany's new school friends are here."

A gentle warmth spread through Ella's chest. If she'd learned anything about Luke over the past few weeks, it was that he valued Bethany's happiness and well-being more than anything else—even the rink. The building could probably crumble to the ground around them, and as long as his niece had a smile on her face, he'd still be a happy man.

Just what she needed. Another reason to keep falling for him.

Her hand tightened around Snickers's leash, and the dog looked up at her with his furry forehead creased. Ella gave him a reassuring pat. *No need to worry, bud. Everything is fine.*

But then, all of a sudden, it wasn't.

When Luke was a kid, he and his younger brother, Steven, had always been fascinated by domino chains. Whenever the weather got too bad to head outside—as it sometimes did during the snowy Alaskan winters—they spent long hours arranging neat rows of dominos through-out the house. Luke's role in this activity had always been that of the ambitious architect. He'd make outlandish suggestions like snaking the dominos down the staircase, arranging them in a spiral pattern, or making a long train that started on the fireplace mantel and then cascaded onto the floor, ultimately stretching through multiple rooms.

Somehow Steven always made it happen. Luke's brother had been blessed with the kind of meticulous patience and attention to detail that he'd never mastered. While Luke thought up elaborate setups, Steven did the painstaking work of making them a reality, setting each domino in place, spaced just right. But in the end, when they tapped the first domino in the chain and watched the others fall, it always felt like a true team effort—possibly the only thing that Luke and Steven actually worked on together... the only thing they'd ever had in common.

So when Luke noticed the way Gran's face lit up in the middle of the grand reopening party, eyes fixed on the rink's entrance and that balloon arch he'd sweated over for more hours than he wanted to count, he should've recognized the moment for what it was: the first tap in a long row of dominos. A gentle push that set in motion a chain reaction that could only be described as a spectacular disaster.

"You made it," Gran said, her attention still fixed on the entrance as she clapped her hands and bustled toward Luke. "Luke, honey, look who's here."

He turned his head, clueless but intrigued. Then he felt his smile die on his lips as his gaze landed on the middle-aged couple who'd just walked through the door of his ice rink.

"Mom?" He swallowed, eyes shifting toward his father. "Dad?"

His parents were here? They'd come all the way from

Oregon to attend his grand reopening party? How had they even known about it? Their weekly video calls were perfunctory at best. Luke always had the feeling they were going through the motions speaking with him, putting in the time to be polite before asking him to turn the monitor over to Bethany. He hadn't talked to them about the rink at all. The last thing he'd wanted to do was draw unwanted attention toward an ill-conceived real-estate investment that had nearly bankrupted him.

Don't count your chickens before they hatch, a voice in the back of his head warned. Or, as they said in hockey, "don't start celebrating before the puck drops." This place could still end up bankrupting him in the long run. Today was a start, that's all.

"I thought your parents might want to be here to help celebrate your new business venture," Gran said as she patted his arm. Bless her heart, she'd been trying for all of Luke's life to mend the rocky relationship between him and his dad. She wasn't going to give up anytime soon, apparently.

"Hello, son," his father said, extending his hand as if he were greeting a professional contact instead of his only surviving child. "Your grandmother called a few days ago and invited us to your party. We had no idea."

Luke took his dad's hand and tried not to feel like a little kid being picked up from hockey practice. He was still here, hanging out at the rink of his youth, while Steven had gone on to bigger and better things.

Go easy on them. They're here. They're trying. Shouldn't you try, too?

His mother greeted him with cordial detachment—or maybe that was just Luke's imagination. In any event, he thanked both his parents for making the trip.

"I'll go grab Bethany. She'll be thrilled to see you both," Luke said. Then he turned toward Ella, standing quietly at his side. "You remember Ella Grace, don't you?"

Mom's face creased into a broad smile as she toyed with the buttons on her sweater set. She and Dad both looked like they were dressed for an afternoon at a country club instead of a drafty old skating rink in small-town Alaska. It had clearly been a while since they'd visited Snowhaven. Luke wondered when they'd last made a trip to visit Gran. Then again, who was he to talk? He was hardly a perfect example of family values.

"Of course," his mother said, nodding at Ella. "Travis's little sister."

Ella's smile went strained around the edges for a beat—just for a second, though. Luke doubted anyone else noticed how being referred to as her brother's kid sister rankled. She had, after all, grown up and made something of herself.

"Ella runs a fantastic dog-training business here in town. They provide guide dogs and service dogs to people in need of support," Luke said.

"Interesting. Is this one of them?" Dad asked, glancing down at Snickers, who'd chosen this most inopportune moment to stretch out on the floor and gnaw on Ella's shoelaces.

Clink went the second domino in the chain.

Ella's cheeks went pink as she shook the dog off. "Snickers, no," she whispered, smile freezing into place as she nodded at his father. "No, actually. Snickers here was one of our trainees, but now he's my pet. He wasn't as suited for the program as we'd initially hoped. But there are some other amazing dogs here from Helping

Hounds if you'd like to meet them, including Bethany's sweet companion, Cupcake."

"Ah, Cupcake. We've certainly heard a lot about that little pup," Mom said.

"She and Bethany make a great pair," Ella said just as the little girl joined their semi-awkward group, eyes widening at the sight of her grandparents.

"Excuse me, are you Mr. Tanner?" A woman Luke had never met before tapped him on the shoulder. She was about the same age as his parents, with dark hair that fell just past her shoulders. Unlike his mom and dad, she was dressed practically in a weatherproof jacket, cozy knit sweater, and hiking boots. Her voice sounded vaguely familiar. "I'm Elaine Miller from Snowhaven Realty."

Right, the real estate agent who'd facilitated his long-distance purchase of the rink. Luke nodded while Bethany introduced his parents to Cupcake and Ella made small talk with Gran. "It's nice to finally meet you in person, Elaine."

"I can't believe what you've done with this place. I'm so impressed." The woman held her arms open wide, encompassing their surroundings. "I had to come down here and see it for myself, especially after the call I got about thirty minutes ago."

Clink went the third domino.

"What call?" Luke asked. Should he have known what she was talking about? Keeping up with this conversation was difficult when his attention was being pulled in multiple directions.

"The call with the offer." She flashed him a triumphant grin. "I'm here to tell you that your efforts have paid off. The refurbishment has attracted a lot of attention here in town. As I mentioned when we talked recently, I didn't expect you to be able to sell the rink, but I put some feelers out and this morning, the impossible happened. A buyer just made a cash offer, and it's quite generous—enough to cover your original purchase price of the rink, plus go a long way toward recouping your investment in the improvements you've made."

Ella's gaze flicked toward him from a few feet away. Clearly, she'd overheard everything.

"You're selling the rink?" she blurted.

"No." Luke shook his head, eyes shifting back toward Elaine Miller from Snowhaven Realty. "I mean, probably not."

"I didn't realize it was for sale," Ella said, and his heart twisted as she buried her fingers into Snickers's chocolate-colored fur.

She was upset, and he didn't blame her one bit. They'd spent so much time together since he'd been back, and he'd never mentioned he was thinking about selling. Because he wasn't…not anymore. However, a generous cash offer sounded like something he should consider.

That was the responsible thing to do, right?

"It's not for sale. Not officially," he said, digging the hole he was in even deeper.

"But you are interested in the offer, aren't you? You sounded desperate to sell when we talked on the phone," the real estate agent said.

Clink, clink, clink. The dominoes were falling faster than Luke could count them.

Bethany glanced back and forth between him and Ella, her innocent face creased with worry. "What's wrong?" she signed. "Why are you guys mad at each other?"

"We're not mad, sweetheart," Ella signed.

"I should think not." Luke's mother huffed. "This is the

best news Luke could possibly get. Now, you can get out from under this place and bring Bethany back to Oregon."

"What?" Bethany turned to Luke, her wide blue eyes brimming with worry. Cupcake craned her neck and began to lick Bethany's fingertips. "We're leaving?"

Luke felt like he was being dragged underwater and he'd forgotten how to swim.

"You know it's the right thing, son," his father said quietly. "It's what Steven would've wanted. He chose to raise his daughter there, and we're certain he expected you to do the same."

Bethany fidgeted with the frilly trim of her apron. They'd found it a few days ago in one of the kitchen drawers at the cottage, and she'd been so excited to wear it to the party. Gran had altered it for her by hand just yesterday.

"Please don't fight," Bethany said in a small voice. "Why is everyone so mad?"

Cupcake nudged closer to Luke's precious niece, pawing at her legs as tears filled her eyes. Bethany started to cry, her chest rising and falling as she struggled to catch her breath.

"Luke, I think Bethany might be having an anxiety attack," Ella said evenly. "Maybe we should all calm down and get her seated?"

"Come here, sweetheart," Luke said, gathering Bethany into his arms as he carried her to one of the benches for patrons to get in and out of their skates. Out of the corner of his eye, he spotted the girls from Bethany's class, openly staring.

Were the girls going to ostracize Bethany at school now? Was he going to have another bullying situation on his hands?

"Try and take deep breaths," he murmured, rubbing his hand in gentle circles over Bethany's back. "You're okay, sweetheart. I promise."

"Luke, you really need to get that dog to stop licking her hand like that. It's not sanitary," his mother said as she reached toward Cupcake.

"Mrs. Tanner, Cupcake is just doing her job. She's trying to soothe Bethany and reassure her that she's okay. Please don't intervene," Ella said.

"Son, do something," Luke's dad said. "The child is distressed."

"Cupcake, no!" his mom said, obviously still hung up on germs. Luke was starting to remember why he and Steven had never been allowed to have a pet as kids. "Come here."

"Mrs. Tanner, it's okay. Cupcake isn't going to hurt her, and the dog can't hear you. She's deaf," Ella said, but even her usually calm demeanor was beginning to crumble.

"Don't take my dog!" Bethany screamed.

Dad turned sharp eyes on Luke. "Are you going to let her speak to your mother like that? She never had tantrums like this when Steven was alive. What exactly has been going on around here?"

"She's not having a tantrum, Dad. She's having an anxiety attack," Luke said, and if everyone didn't calm down, he was probably going to have one, too.

"I'm going to go," Elaine Miller said gently. Luke had forgotten the real estate agent was still there. Likewise, he'd forgotten he was in the middle of a party. Although, he could see people drifting toward the exit in his periphery. "Give me a call when you have a chance."

She pressed her business card into Luke's hand. He shoved it in his pocket.

"Uncle Luke, please. Don't let Grandma and Grandpa take Cupcake away from me!" Bethany wailed. Her speaking voice, which had never come easy, had devolved until it was nearly unintelligible.

"I won't, sweetie," he promised.

But the damage was done, All he could do was take her in his arms and close his eyes while the final domino teetered and then fell.

An hour later—or possibly a century, since Luke had lost all sense of time and reason—the skating rink had emptied out. Ella and her crew had packed up the dogs and gone back to Helping Hounds. Travis had helped usher the party patrons out of the building with promises for free skating sessions in the coming week to give Bethany a chance to recover from her anxiety attack in private. Then he'd given Gran, Bethany, and Cupcake a ride back to Snowhaven Assisted Living so Luke could have a heart-to-heart alone with his parents.

It was the last place on earth he wanted to be, but it was time to face the music.

"Luke, I'm sorry," his mother said, and he had to give her credit. She seemed genuinely apologetic. "I didn't realize Cupcake's licking behavior was therapeutic. I was only trying to help. Bethany was so upset, and I think I just panicked."

"It's okay, Mom," Luke said. He wished things hadn't devolved the way they had, but he got it. He'd panicked, too. He'd never seen Bethany like that before.

This is all your fault. You heard what Dad said. Nothing like this ever happened while Steven was alive.

Luke lifted weary eyes to his father. "I'm sorry, Dad."

He wasn't altogether sure what he was apologizing

for—everything, possibly. He was sorry they'd come all the way from Oregon to witness his disaster of a party. He was sorry Bethany was hurting. Most of all, he was sorry he wasn't Steven.

"Listen, son. We're not upset. We're just concerned—for you as well as Bethany," Dad said.

He was sitting on one of the benches in the lobby directly opposite the one where Luke sat. And all at once, Luke realized he couldn't remember his father darkening the door of the skating rink before. Not even for one of his hockey games when he was a kid. No wonder the man looked so woefully out of place.

"I'm worried about Bethany, too," Luke said quietly. How was it possible to sound so calm when his insides were screaming? "I know you didn't get to see it, but she's happy here. I promise."

His parents exchanged a look.

"I know you believe that, but kids hold things inside, Luke. You're new to being a parent, but we raised two wonderful, well-adjusted boys. Trust me when I say that Bethany isn't adapting to Alaska as well as you think she is," his mother said.

And how would you know that, exactly? You haven't even been here a full day. Luke bit down hard on his tongue. He couldn't—*shouldn't*—say things like that. Because his parents were right. He didn't know the right way to care for Bethany, did he? He'd been doing his best to give her everything she needed, but maybe his best wasn't good enough.

"Steven left Bethany to you, and we accept that now, son," Dad said in an uncharacteristically tender tone. "But that doesn't mean you don't need our help. We've cleared out the guesthouse, and we want you and Bethany to move in. That way she has her entire family close by, and she'll be the most loved little girl in the entire world."

But what about Gran? And Ella…and everyone else who Bethany cared about in Snowhaven. They were her family, too.

"You have to admit, the offer on the rink came at the perfect time. Nothing is keeping you here now. You and Bethany can move back home right away." His mother smiled as if the suggestion was already a foregone conclusion. "And don't worry—Cupcake is welcome to join you."

Was he supposed to fall down on his knees with gratitude now? His parents were both looking at him as if he should.

He dragged a hand through his hair, unsure what to say as the door to the rink opened, and someone stepped inside.

"Sorry, it's just me." Ella's friend Molly waved as she grabbed a bundle of fabric off the floor near the entrance. "I forgot my scarf."

Luke waved back. He didn't have the energy to say anything. This entire conversation had stolen his ability to form words.

Maybe because deep down, you know they might be right.

"It's settled then." Luke's father stood. "Your mother and I are heading to the airport in Anchorage. There's no reason to stay. You're doing the right thing, Luke. Let's try and get everything wrapped up as quickly as possible, okay? The sooner you sign the paperwork and the sale goes through, the sooner you and Bethany can come on home."

Home?

Luke nodded, but he was still hung up on that one word—home.

Where was that, exactly?

Luke sat alone at his desk and dropped his head in his hands, tugging at the ends of his hair until his scalp stung.

Please, God. Tell me what to do.

If he'd gotten an offer on the rink two weeks ago— possibly even two *days* ago—he would've jumped at the chance to unload it. Now, though, he wasn't sure he could. He'd poured his blood, sweat, and tears into this place trying to get ready for the big grand reopening. And against all odds, he'd actually done it.

He'd had some help, of course. Without Travis and Ella, he never would've been able to pull it off. Travis had put in almost as much physical labor as Luke had, and Ella…well, Ella had pulled off the impossible. She'd gotten the local press to cover the refurbishment efforts. She'd posted flyers about the grand reopening all over town. She'd brought service dogs to his party. What better way to attract a crowd?

More importantly, though, Ella had made him believe— not just in the rink, but in *himself*. Without her, he'd have probably thrown in the towel. Because of Ella, when he looked around the ramshackle building, he no longer saw a run-down ice rink that had lost its shine. He saw a place where the past and the present could come together and make something new. Something precious. A place where kids could come and learn to skate, where they could grow strong and confident, where the town could gather and rally around their own.

And maybe, just maybe, he saw a future for himself that he hadn't dared to imagine before.

All of that had come crashing down when Bethany had her anxiety attack. Luke had felt like he'd stepped right out of a blissful dream—warm, safe, and full of promise—straight into a nightmare. He'd never forget the lost look in Bethany's eyes when she'd begged him to not let her grandparents take her dog away. As if she'd really thought he'd allow that to happen. She'd done so well since they'd moved to Snowhaven. She had friends here. She had Cupcake and Ella and Gran.

Luke's parents hadn't seen any of that, though. All they'd seen was a worried little girl whose world had cracked beneath her feet like thin ice during the first thaw. In an instant, everything good and secure had splintered apart and she'd plunged into cold uncertainty.

Were his mom and dad right? Would he and Bethany be better off living with them in Oregon?

Luke didn't want to believe that any more than he wanted to sell the ice rink, but the timing of the offer seemed awfully serendipitous. He had an out now. He could walk away, free and clear. When Ella found Cupcake at the shelter, she'd told him she believed it had all been part of God's plan. What if *this* was God's plan, too? Maybe that's why it had all come together so easily. The pieces were all falling into place, like one of Gran's jigsaw puzzles.

Is it a sign? He squeezed his eyes shut tight. *God, is this really You?*

A noise broke through the silence—the opening of a door, followed by rapid footsteps. Luke jerked his head up, pulse hammering, just as Ella stormed into his office.

She'd been crying. Her pretty, porcelain face was stained with tears, but the fury in her eyes burned through the sadness, raw and fierce.

"Tell me it's not true," she said in a trembling voice.

Luke hesitated. "Ella—"

"Tell me you're not selling the rink and moving to Oregon." Her eyes moved frantically over his face, searching his expression for clues. "Tell me, Luke."

"Where did you hear I was moving to Oregon, Elly Bean?" he asked with exaggerated calm. If she would just give him time to explain, surely she'd understand.

Understand what, exactly? That you're bailing on everything she's helped you build here in Snowhaven?

"Molly told me. I was standing right there when you got the offer on the rink, but I never imagined you'd take it. She said you're selling and taking Bethany to live with your parents." Ella glared at him. "And do *not* call me Elly Bean right now."

Luke sighed. *Of course.* He should've seen this coming. Molly, the receptionist from Helping Hounds, had come back to the rink to collect her forgotten scarf, and she'd apparently heard everything—or at least enough to understand that Luke already had one foot out the door.

"I'm sorry. I didn't want you to hear about this from anyone but me." He held up his hands and stood, but when he walked closer to Ella, her posture grew even more rigid.

He was messing up this conversation, just like he messed up everything else.

"So it's true." She huffed out an incredulous laugh. "You're really doing it. You're walking away again, just like you did last time. Were you planning on telling me goodbye, or were you going to disappear into thin air like you did before?"

Luke's jaw clenched. They'd come so far, only to end up right back here again. He looked around at the freshly painted walls, done in the same colors as his childhood hockey jersey, and the past decade seemed to melt away like yesterday's snow. He was breaking Ella Grace's heart all over again.

"It's not like that," he said.

"Then what's it like, Luke? You promised Bethany a home. You *kissed* me—almost, anyway. And now what? You're running?" She threw her hands in the air. "Look, I know how rattled you were when your parents showed up. I could see the hesitation all over your face. But you handled it. And when Bethany got upset, you handled that, too. I told you there would be ups and downs with her anxiety. She's still grieving, but Cupcake is helping her. You don't have to go."

He looked away, because he couldn't take the pain in her eyes anymore. Then the silence stretched between them until Luke felt like he might suffocate.

"I haven't made up my mind yet," he said without meeting her gaze.

But they both knew it was a lie. Hadn't he just been sitting here, convincing himself that packing up and leaving was all part of God's plan? He was tired...so very tired. He'd been stumbling around in the dark, trying to be a parent, when he didn't have the first clue what Bethany really needed. He'd moved her all the way to Alaska on a whim. He'd mismanaged his finances so badly that his credit card got declined in front of her teacher. Today she'd been so upset that she'd had a meltdown in front of her new friends, and Luke had been powerless to help.

Shame flooded over him, leaving him cold. If moving away was the right thing to do, why did it feel so wrong? Weren't his days of running from his problems and hopping from place to place supposed to be over?

"I should've known this was going to happen," Ella said. She was dry-eyed now, which should've been a relief. Luke had caused her enough tears for a lifetime already. But somehow, the emptiness in her gaze cut deeper than a sob ever could.

She was done with him. Finished. She'd promised him she wouldn't fall in love, and he'd made that vow all too easy to keep. He had no one to blame for this mess but himself.

"Goodbye, Luke," she said in a hollow voice he didn't recognize.

Everything was happening too fast. He closed his eyes, dizzy and numb from the shock of it all. He couldn't let her give up on him. If she walked away now, he'd probably never see her again.

"Ella, wait—" he said, and his voice broke as he called her name.

But it was too late. When at long last, he opened his eyes, his Elly Bean was already gone.

Chapter Fifteen

Ella left the rink fully intending to go home. All she wanted to do was hug Snickers around his warm, soft neck and cry her eyes out. But she knew once she started, she might never stop, so instead of driving back to her cottage, she steered her car toward the one place where she could safely revel in her anger.

"Ella? What are you doing here?" Travis's face creased with concern as he took in the messy sight of her. Judging by the alarm written all over his face, she looked like a complete and utter disaster. "Come in. What's wrong? Did something happen?"

Ruby gave Ella a wary sniff as she crossed the threshold. Wonderful. Even her brother's dog could smell her heartache. She probably reeked of it.

Ella petted Ruby and told her everything was okay, but the husky didn't seem to buy it. Once they sat down at the farm table, she stuck close to Travis's side as if she could somehow protect him from whatever was ailing Ella.

"Luke is selling the ice rink. He and Bethany are moving back to Oregon," she said flatly. There was just no way to sugarcoat it.

"But Luke doesn't even get along with his parents. You know that. He didn't exactly look thrilled when they showed up at the party," Travis said. "That can't be right. Plus, we just got the rink opened up."

"None of it makes sense, but it's true. I just came from the rink. He's walking away, Trav. Just like he did before." Tears burned at the backs of Ella's eyes but she blinked them away. She refused to fall apart here, in front of her brother. She could cry herself dehydrated later, in the privacy of her own home.

"I didn't see this coming. Not even after what happened today." Travis drew in a long breath. "I really thought he was here to stay."

She'd expected him to get angry—maybe even be more furious than she was. Travis and Luke had been best friends for even longer than her hero worship of Luke had turned into something more. Something real.

But Travis didn't seem mad at all. As she sat there fuming, her brother just looked unspeakably sad.

"It's just like last time," she repeated. Was he not listening? Where was the indignation?

Travis shook his head. "You've got it wrong, Ella."

She let out a haughty laugh. "No, I don't. I told you I just came from the ice rink. You should see him. He looks…" *Heartbroken*, she realized with a pang. She knew that look. She'd seen it in the mirror for months after the love-letter humiliation.

Ella took a deep breath and tried to erase the image of Luke looking so crestfallen clear out of her head. It wasn't helping matters at all. What she needed right now was to feel furious. The second she stopped, she'd fall apart. Even her sweet Snickers might not be able to put her back together.

"Never mind how he looked. That's not important. You should've heard him. He tried to tell me he hadn't made up his mind yet, but I can tell he already has. He and Bethany will probably be gone before the sun comes up." She couldn't believe that Travis was still just sitting there, as calm as could be. He'd put so much work in at the rink—nearly as much as Luke had, and her brother normally spent all his free time at the log house in the woods. Sometimes she even joked that he had the social skills of a bear fresh out of hibernation. It didn't make a bit of sense why he wouldn't be upset.

"That's not what I meant, sis." Travis's eyes locked onto hers. "You've got it wrong about the past. It didn't happen the way you think it did."

A frown tugged at Ella's lips. What was he talking about? "He up and left, Travis. He never told me goodbye. I know you two were best friends, and I was just your annoying kid sister back then, but Luke meant something to me. It hurt when he disappeared like that."

"I know it hurt, which is why I never told you that I'm the reason he left town the way he did," her brother said quietly. His gaze dropped to his hands, folded loosely on the table.

He was eerily still. *Too* still. There was clearly more to this story, and Ella was almost afraid to ask what he was holding back.

But if she didn't get the whole truth now, after a decade had passed, she never would. "That doesn't make any sense, Trav. You two were so close. You loved him like a brother. What could you have possibly done to make him go?"

"We had a fight." Travis winced. "A bad one. I told him I never wanted to see him again, and I told him if he ever went near you again, I'd kill him."

Ella couldn't believe what she was hearing. Her entire

world seemed to tilt as her brother looked at her, eyes full of unspoken history.

"Say something," he said. "Please?"

"Wh-why would you do that?" she choked out, but she knew. She just didn't want to believe it.

Travis knew about the love letters. Humiliation burned anew. She felt like she might forget how to swallow...or breathe. *He's known this entire time.*

"I found a letter you wrote to him," Travis said woodenly. "The night before graduation I was out late with some friends. I got home past curfew, and when I was sneaking in, I found it, facedown in the snow. Luke's name was written on the front of the envelope in your handwriting, and I couldn't figure out why you would've written my best friend a letter."

"So you *read* it?" Ella said in such a loud voice that Ruby's mismatched eyes went narrow. The Siberian inched closer to Travis. If Ella had been anyone else, the dog might've even growled at her.

But Ruby knew Ella. She'd just never heard her raise her voice before.

"I'm sorry. I was an idiot, okay? I guess on some level I must've picked up on the fact that you had a crush on Luke." Travis scrubbed his face with both hands and groaned. "Believe me, I wish I hadn't read it."

"That makes two of us," Ella muttered, face burning.

"I jumped to some conclusions that might not have been correct. I thought you and Luke must have been a secret couple or something. He was so much older than you. I just lost it." Travis sat back in his chair and shook his head. "I'm sorry."

"It was never like that between Luke and me," Ella said. *Until now...*

But it still wasn't like that. Not really. If Luke loved her the way she loved him, he'd never just up and leave.

Am I genuinely in love with him? She turned the question over in her head, but there was really no need. She'd fallen for Luke all over again, and this time, she was adult enough to know what those feelings meant.

"Luke tried to tell me you were just friends and it was only a crush, but I didn't believe him." Her brother released a long, tortured exhale. "So, like I said, it's my fault he left without saying goodbye."

"I don't understand." Ella shook her head. "Why are you telling me this now, after all this time?"

"Because you need to know that Luke isn't the type of man who just walks away from someone he cares deeply about. That's not him. It never was," Travis said, and the earnestness in his expression was impossible to ignore.

Did the past really matter so much, though, when it didn't change a thing about the present?

"You're wrong about that," she countered. "That's exactly what he's doing."

Travis folded his arms over his chest, and the way his eyes narrowed made him look so much like Ruby that it was almost comical. Ella might have laughed if she didn't feel so much like crying. "Tell me something. When you went over there just now, did you tell him how you really feel? Does he know you love him?"

"But I don't love him," she said. Maybe if she repeated it enough times, it would be true.

"Come on, Ella. I'm not blind. I know love when I see it. Luke has feelings for you, too. I knew it from the moment I saw you on the ice together. You two are in love." He gave her a small smile and said, "It's written all over both your faces every time you're around each other."

"We're not," she insisted. If Luke was in love with her, he would tell her. He would *stay*.

Not if you pushed him away, just like Travis did all those years ago.

Was that what she'd done tonight? Had she been so ready to hear bad news that she'd lashed out without giving him a chance to explain?

Guilty as charged. There was a reason the phrase *be still* was repeated so many times in the Bible. She should've waited to hear him out, but she'd been so afraid of getting hurt again that she'd done the exact opposite. She'd hurt him before he had the chance.

"Yes, you are, and it's okay. You and Luke belong together. I didn't want to believe it at first, but you do. Anyone who's spent any time around the two of you can see it." He hesitated for a beat and reached into the pocket of his flannel shirt. "I'd planned on giving this to Luke today. I didn't want him to think I didn't approve—not that you guys need my permission or anything. I just wanted him to know that I saw what was happening and that I understood. You're meant for each other. Anyway, things at the party spiraled before I had a chance…"

Her brother gently placed a small wooden carving on the table, and Ella felt as if all the air had been knocked out of her body.

She blinked, struggling to make sense of what she was seeing. The carving looked so much like the others, whittled from soft silver spruce, each knot and curve carefully formed. Like the most recent ones, it also told a story… A story so intricate and beautiful that it made Ella's heart ache anew—two bald eagles, in mid-flight with their talons locked and wings outstretched.

She'd seen bald eagles do this before over the Kenai

River. The first time had been when she, Travis, and Luke had gone on a dogsledding day trip with Dad. The three of them sat in the basket of the sled, shoulder-to-shoulder, while Dad led the dog team along the snowy riverbank. Ella could still remember the feel of the cold wind on her face, the sound of the dogs' soft footfalls, and the swish of the runners over the frosty terrain.

"Whoa," Dad had called, prompting the dogs to come to a stop as soon as he'd seen the eagles tumbling through the sky over the water. "Look, kids. The eagles are cartwheeling."

It had looked like an exquisite dance. They'd twisted and turned, locked together, gracefully spiraling down, down, down, only letting go at the last possible moment before they hit the swirling dark water.

"Cartwheeling?" Ella had echoed.

"That's what their courtship ritual is called," Dad explained. "It's how bald eagles fall in love, and once they do, they stay together for life."

They'd stayed by the river for nearly half an hour, transfixed as the majestic birds tumbled through the sky together, over and over again. It was one of Ella's core memories of growing up in Alaska, and she had no doubt that Travis and Luke remembered that day, too.

"It's supposed to be you and Luke," Travis said gently.

"I don't know what to say." A lump lodged in the back of Ella's throat that made speaking nearly impossible, but suddenly there was so much to unpack. Memories, old and new.

She picked up the eagle carving and traced their finely carved feathers with reverent fingertips. It was the most beautiful piece of art she'd ever seen—so much like Dad's but at the same time, even more masterful. More *meaningful*.

All this time, Travis had been the mystery whittler. Ella couldn't believe she hadn't seen it. The signs had been there all along—the pocketknife on the mantel in the same spot where Dad had kept his, the way Travis had gone so quiet after each new discovery, his reluctance to speculate about the artist's identity, the fact that the initial moose carving had been the only one that hadn't been purposefully placed for someone in their immediate circle to find… Once the cat had been let out of the bag and the family discovered that someone was taking up where Dad left off, Travis had sent personal messages to each of them in meticulously carved wood. Silver spruce from their own backyard.

She should've known. Maybe, on some deeper level, she had, but she'd wanted to hold on to the secret just a little bit longer. Because for a little while, it had been like having her father back.

"You're just full of secrets, aren't you?" she said, gaze sliding back to her brother.

"I was going to tell you about the carvings. I promise. At first, I was just tinkering around. I'd been thinking about Dad a lot." Travis swallowed. "Missing him. And I thought it would be nice to follow in his footsteps in that way. He brought so much unexpected joy to the community with those things. But then you showed up at dinner with the moose, and I figured I should say something."

"Then why didn't you?" Ella asked. She was trying to understand, but there was so much to wrap her head around after this conversation that she didn't know where to start.

"Because Mom called it a holy whisper. She seemed

so happy, and I didn't want to take that away from her—not with the anniversary of Dad's passing bearing down on us." He offered her a sad smile.

Ella gasped. "It's today, isn't it? I knew it was coming, but with the grand reopening of the ice rink, I forgot."

Travis reached for her hand and squeezed it tight. "That's a good thing, Ella. Dad wouldn't want you to dwell on his passing—he'd want you to celebrate his life instead."

"That's what you've been doing." She let her gaze fall on the carving again. "With these."

"I was going to come clean today—to you and Luke, at least. I'm not sure Mom is ready to give up her holy whispers quite yet," Travis said, and then he released her hand and buried his fingers in the thick ruff of fur around Ruby's neck.

A holy whisper. Ella's throat went impossibly tight as she took a moment to study the eagles again. Their cartwheel was a thing of beauty. She wondered what it would be like to let herself go like that. To give herself to Luke and take a leap.

The intertwined bald eagles were meant to be a holy whisper, but their courtship ritual felt more like a scream.

What are you waiting for? they seemed to say. *Go tell Luke how you feel.*

"Luke, I'm so, so sorry." Gran held the door open wide and ushered him into her room at Snowhaven Assisted Living. "I feel like everything that happened today was all my fault."

"Gran, no. Don't blame yourself. None of it was your fault," Luke said, and then he wrapped his grandmother in a tight embrace.

He wasn't typically a hugger. Throughout his adult life, he'd probably given more accidental black eyes during hockey games than he had hugs. Which was obviously indicative of a far bigger problem.

But that's why he was here, wasn't it? To set things right.

"I invited your mom and dad to the grand opening because I was so proud of the life you've built here. I thought it would be a nice surprise. I wanted them to see for themselves what a wonderful father you are to Bethany," Gran said as he released her, clutching at the collar of her bathrobe.

Guilt tugged at him when he noticed she was already dressed for bed. It was late. He'd wasted a lot of time at the rink tonight—time that he should've spent with Bethany instead of wrestling with God when he already knew what his path forward should look like.

"Is she asleep already?" he asked under his breath.

Gran tipped her head in the direction of the attached bedroom. The door was cracked just enough for him to make out the little girl's sleeping form in the semidarkness. A night-light bathed the small room in a golden glow. Luke spotted Cupcake nestled in the crook of Bethany's neck. Ever present, ever true.

He'd made too many mistakes recently—mistakes he was determined to make up for, no matter how long it took. But adopting the sweet Cavalier King Charles spaniel wasn't one of them, no matter what his parents thought. It might've been the best decision he'd ever made, and like so many of the blessings that had found their way to him since he'd come to Snowhaven, that choice had been a direct result of Ella's kindness.

His throat clogged with emotion as he turned his attention back toward his grandmother. "I'm not sure you should refer to me as Bethany's father, Gran. Dad wouldn't like that."

The older woman's eyes flashed. "Well, your father's not here now, is he?"

Luke offered her a smile that tasted bittersweet on his lips. "No, he's not."

"And you're my grandson so I get to call you whatever I choose." Her gray hair didn't budge, sprayed into its usual helmet as she gave a firm nod. "Understood?"

"Yes, ma'am," Luke said.

"Bethany is going to be okay, Luke. Kids bounce back. She's come such a long way since you got here. Today was a little hiccup, that's all. You'll see."

Luke loved his grandmother with his whole heart. Always had. When he'd been younger, his parents' disapproval had clouded his perception of everything. It was hard for him to understand—and even more difficult to admit—that he'd spent years thinking he didn't have a safe place to land when, in reality, he'd had a home all along. Right here with Gran. He only wished it hadn't taken a full decade and one incredibly awkward grand reopening party to realize it.

"Where have you been all night, dear? I've been worried about you." She lowered herself gingerly into her favorite recliner and gestured for Luke to take a seat in the other one.

He shook his head. "I'm actually not staying. I have something important to take care of, and I need to leave Bethany here while I do it, if that's okay. I just wanted to check in on both of you first."

Gran cast him a curious look. "Of course, it's okay. What are you up to, Luke?"

"I needed to do some thinking and make some important decisions. I want to discuss them with you soon—very soon." He owed his grandmother an explanation. She'd offered him her house and all her support when he'd brought Bethany here. Whether or not he sold the rink, whether he stayed or left, those choices would affect his grandmother as much as they impacted his niece.

"That sounds very mysterious," Gran said, regarding him with quiet interest.

"Can I ask you a question?" Luke shifted from one foot to the other. "Do you really think I'm the one who should be raising Bethany?"

He respected Gran's opinion about this, maybe even more than his parents'. He wasn't sure he'd realized how much he'd wanted to make his grandmother proud until today.

"I want you to tell me the truth," he pleaded, his tone raw with emotion.

"Of course, I do. There's no doubt in my mind that she belongs with you, Luke. And there isn't a single reason why anyone should believe otherwise, either. Is that what you've been wrestling with? Have you been asking God for a sign?" Her eyebrows crept closer to her hairline.

He looked at her askance. "How did you know?"

"Because I've known you since you were a baby, Luke. Also, it's what people do when they're feeling desperate for answers. But you don't need a sign, dear. You've already got one. It's been there all along."

Despite everything—despite the empty feeling he'd had since the second his parents had walked through the door of the rink, despite the way Bethany had crumbled when a stranger showed up claiming to be her mother, despite losing Ella—his heart jerked at the words his grandmother had just uttered. It stirred with something bigger than he dared to dream of. Hope. "It has?"

"Yes, sir, it has. The only sign you really need is the one that Steven left for you. You hold your brother in such high regard, sweetheart, and he could've chosen anyone in this world to raise his daughter if something happened to him. Look who he chose." Gran's face cracked into a gentle smile, and her eyes filled. "Steven chose *you*, Luke. That's your sign."

Something unlocked inside of Luke's chest at that moment. He felt like he could breathe again—cool, clear air that washed away the weight he'd been carrying for so long. "You have no idea how bad I needed to hear that, Gran."

"Happy to help, dear." She checked the time on the cuckoo clock and tutted. "Shouldn't you be on your way to this urgent errand of yours?"

Luke shifted again on his feet, voice hopeful but uncertain. "I should, but there's one more thing I need first, Gran. A favor, and it's a big one."

A tender smile spread across her face as she looked at him, and he had a feeling she already knew what he wanted. When had his wise grandmother turned into such a mind reader?

She winked. "Anything for my grandson."

Ella held the cartwheeling eagles snug against her heart as she made her way across the Snowhaven Assisted Living parking lot. Patches of snow dotted the dark asphalt, and if she wasn't careful, she was going to wipe out and twist an ankle. She was in a terrible hurry, though. Nearly an hour had passed since she'd left Travis's house, and she couldn't seem to find Luke anywhere.

She'd gone directly to the ice rink after leaving her brother's place, but the building had been locked up tight. She'd tried peering inside the windows for signs of life, but not a single light was on inside. Then she'd tried knocking for good measure, but that had proven fruitless. Luke wasn't there anymore, and she'd had the sinking feeling that he might not ever show his face there again.

Had he already accepted the offer? Had he told Bethany they were moving back to Oregon? Did his grandmother know yet?

Questions kept tumbling through her mind, and she did her best to ignore them. All that mattered now was finding Luke. The answers would come in due time. She might not like them, but Travis had been right. Luke deserved to know how she felt about him before he left town. Putting her heart on the line and confessing she was in love with him wouldn't be easy, given their history, but she had to do it. She *wanted* to. She just had to find him first...

Ella had tried looking for him at his gran's old cottage in the Gold Rush district immediately after searching for him at the rink, but no one had been there, either. She knocked on the front door so many times that her knuckles were still red and raw from the effort, but Luke had never come to the door. There was only one place in town left to look, hence her mad dash across the assisted-living community's parking lot.

Ella's heart thudded as she pulled open the lobby door and raced past the reception desk. It was empty, of course. The console television in the lobby was turned off, and there wasn't a soul sitting in the lounge area, where the residents usually gathered to play board games, assemble puzzles, or socialize. The place was so quiet that she could hear herself breathe.

Are you really going to knock on an elderly woman's door this time of night?

Yes. Yes, she was. Desperate times called for desperate measures. What Ella had to say to Luke couldn't wait until morning. If she didn't stop him, he and Bethany could be halfway to Oregon by the time the sun came up.

The nighttime security guard smiled and waved as she jogged past him toward Luke's grandmother's room. Ella forced herself to slow down before she got there. If she knocked on the older woman's door in such a frantic state, Ella would probably frighten her to death.

She stopped around the corner from Mrs. Tanner's room and tried to catch her breath. *Inhale...exhale.* Ella closed her eyes, leaned her back against the hallway wall, and tried the counting technique they taught clients at Helping Hounds who needed service dogs to help deal with anxiety. But she must've been doing it wrong because instead of feeling more relaxed, something else happened—something weird. She thought she heard someone say her name, and that someone sounded an awful lot like Luke.

"Ella?"

Her eyes flew open, and there he was, standing a mere arm's length away. Luke Tanner, in the flesh.

"Hi," she said, swallowing hard. Now that she'd found him, she wasn't quite sure where to start. All she knew for certain was that she was so relieved to see him that her knees nearly buckled. She was suddenly incredibly grateful for the solid surface of the wall holding her upright. "What are you doing here?"

A lopsided grin flickered across his face. That smile had to be a positive sign, right? As was the fact that he was still here in Snowhaven instead of on the interstate somewhere headed south. "My gran lives here."

"Right. I know that," she said. She was so nervous she couldn't even think straight. Had she been this terrified the last time she confessed her feelings to him? Probably not. She'd been too young and naive to realize how dangerous it was—how much it hurt to tell someone she loved them only to hear they didn't love her back.

Luke took a step closer, his steady gaze locking onto hers. The warmth in his eyes sent a shiver down her spine. "And what are *you* doing here, Elly Bean?"

Joy bloomed inside her like spring after a long Alaskan winter. She'd never been so happy to hear that silly nickname in all her life.

"I came here looking for you." She pushed off the wall, stood up straight on her wobbly legs, and motioned toward his gran's room. "Again."

"This is becoming a habit," Luke said, cocking a single eyebrow. "I think I like it."

Ella laughed, and for a second, she wondered if she needed to say anything at all. Maybe they could just pick up where they left off and pretend the awful discussion at the rink earlier had never happened.

As tempting as that might be, that's not what Ella wanted. She didn't just want to be a part of Luke's life. She wanted it all. She wanted to fly high, take his hand, and then free fall together into life's most beautiful dance. She wanted forever…with him.

"I'm sorry about earlier, Luke. I said a lot of things I had no business saying, and—"

His expression went bittersweet. "Please don't apologize. I'm the one who's sorry. I'm not selling the rink.

Bethany and I are staying right here in Snowhaven. This is our home."

"It is?" Her heart swelled, tender in the best possible way—a new kind of heartache. "Wait, don't say anything else yet, okay? I came here to tell you something. It's what I should've said earlier...the only thing that really matters."

He nodded, lips parting slightly while he waited for her to finish.

"I'm in love with you, Luke. I promised myself it wouldn't happen, but it did, and I'm not even sorry." The words came out in a rush, and once they were out there, she knew she'd never be able to take them back. But she didn't want to, not this time. This time was for keeps.

Luke didn't say anything at first. He didn't have to. The devotion in his eyes said it all as he took her face in his hands and pressed his forehead to hers.

"Don't be sorry. I love you, too, Ella," he whispered, and then he smiled into her eyes just like he'd done on the ice.

His gaze dropped to her mouth and then he kissed her, softly and sweetly. There were no interruptions this time—just the two of them, feet firmly planted in the present. Yesterday no longer mattered anymore.

Ella melted into him, the eagle figurine forgotten until it bumped into his chest. When it did, he pulled away just far enough to glance down at it.

"What's this?" he said as his fingers curled around hers.

She opened her hand to reveal the cartwheeling eagles, delighting in the way Luke's eyes danced as they swept over the meticulously carved birds. He remembered the day by the river when they were kids. She wasn't the only one who'd held on tight to that special memory.

"Travis made it. It's been him all along. He's the mystery whittler," she said, heart full to bursting. "He wanted to give it to you tonight, and he said to tell you that the eagles are us—you and me."

"'This is how they fall in love,'" Luke murmured, quoting her father that morning on the riverbank. "'And once they do, they stay together for life.'"

Then he lifted his gaze back to hers, and before she realized what he was doing, he dropped to one knee at her feet.

"Luke?" Ella's heart thundered in her chest. Was this really happening?

"I wasn't planning on doing this here in my grandmother's retirement home, but I recognize a sign when I see one—just a little something I learned lately." He grinned up at her as he reached into his shirt pocket and pulled out a delicate platinum ring topped with a sparkling diamond. The dazzling center stone was a perfect drop of ice surrounded by tiny diamonds encrusted along the edges. A timeless snowflake. "I came here tonight to ask Gran for this. It's the ring my grandfather gave her back when he proposed, and now—with Gran's blessing, of course—I want it to be yours. Ella Grace, will you marry me?"

She nodded, not quite trusting herself to speak. When she finally managed to make a sound, it came out in a broken whisper. "Yes."

Luke slipped the ring on her finger, stood, and brushed a tear from her cheek that she hadn't realized had fallen. "Don't cry, Elly Bean. It's you and me now. Together forever."

"Forever." She nodded. "Just like the eagles."

"I do have one question first." He grinned, eyes crinkling in the corners. "I'm a little confused. The other day, you taught me that we should all be more like dogs. Now, we're bald eagles. Which is it, future Mrs. Tanner? Am I a dog or an eagle?"

She looked into the ice-blue eyes she'd known and adored for as long as she could remember, and she saw forever stretching out before her. Gloriously wild and unpredictable. *Hold on tight*, her soul whispered, *the free fall starts now*.

"You can be whatever and whoever you want to be, Luke Tanner. So long as you're mine."

Epilogue

One month later...

"**W**ow, Trav." Ella's gaze shifted from the twinkle lights strung over the great stone fireplace to her brother, standing beside her with a coffee cup in his hand and Ruby sitting loyally at his feet, her ears perked like she was listening in. "You decorated and everything."

"It's a party." Travis tipped his head toward the banner hanging from the ceiling's wooden beams. *New Beginnings and Good Dogs Welcome Here*, it read. "You think three life-changing events don't deserve a few strings of lights?"

"Point taken." Ella clinked her mug of cocoa against his and her heart squeezed in that aching way it sometimes did when life surprised her with all its blessings. If she wasn't careful, she was going to cry.

Not now, she told herself. Like Travis said, this was a party. A party celebrating three big things.

The first—Bethany's adoption. Luke was no longer just the little girl's uncle or guardian. He was her father. The papers had arrived just last week, and Luke had been visibly emotional when he'd shown her the official documents. She loved that the one thing that could reduce her big, manly hockey player to tears was the moment he officially became a dad. Since he'd fully committed to life in Alaska, Ella had watched Luke settle into his role as Bethany's father with a newfound confidence. It seemed only right that things were finally official.

The second reason for the party was to celebrate the glittering diamond on Ella's left hand, which still made her breath catch every time it caught the light. *Engaged.* She could hardly believe it, even though they'd wasted no time getting started on wedding plans. The ceremony would take place at Christmas in the little white chapel in downtown Snowhaven, surrounded by everyone they loved. That included the dogs, of course. Travis had offered to walk Ella down the aisle, and she'd taken him up on it, but Snickers was going to make an awfully cute ring bearer. And next weekend, Ella planned on taking Bethany shopping for flower girl dresses in Anchorage. She was certain the florist could make a flower wreath for Cupcake that matched Bethany's bouquet. Sweet, devoted Cupcake, the third reason for the party today.

A few days ago, the little Cavalier had completed her training with flying colors. She was now an official emotional-support dog, with full permission to accompany Bethany to classes at Snowhaven Elementary. Bethany had beamed for two days straight, hands flying with signs about how proud she was and how they needed to throw a party with "at least two kinds of dog biscuits" and her closest friends from school.

Ella had trained a lot of dogs over the years. Some went on to guide, some to comfort, some to assist in ways most people never realized. But Cupcake? She was something else. She watched over Bethany like she was her whole world, responding to her cues with quiet brilliance. That dog didn't just support. She loved.

"Still standing over here with that goofy smile on your face like you're in the middle of a cheesy rom com?" Luke's voice was warm against Ella's ear as he slid an arm around her waist, pulling her close.

She leaned into him, sighing with contentment. "Just soaking it in. I don't want to forget a single second of this."

He pressed a kiss to her temple. "Me neither."

Snow fell like powdered sugar outside the windows, coating the tall pines and silver spruce trees surrounding the cabin. The world felt soft and hushed beyond the frosted glass, but inside was warm, tender chaos.

Bethany sat cross-legged by the coffee table, hands moving in animated bursts as she signed back and forth with her new best friends, Hazel and Lila. Cupcake sat beside her with a lopsided party hat perched between her fluffy ears. Laughter echoed from the kitchen where Gran was attempting to show Luke's father how to decorate sugar cookies. He and Luke's mother had come up from Oregon for the celebration. They were coming to terms with Luke's decision to remain in Alaska, and since arriving for the party, Travis had taken them on a dog sledding excursion, and they'd watched Luke coach the new youth hockey league at the ice rink. Snowhaven was growing on them, dog hair and all.

Ella's mother clapped her hands and beckoned everyone over to the farm table. "All right, everyone. Let's have a look at this cake before someone gets into it early."

She shot a pointed look at Travis, who held up his hands in mock innocence.

"I didn't sneak a bite, I promise. I was just moving it

to a safer place on the counter, like a responsible adult," he said.

"Sure you were," Ella said with a grin.

"Cake sounds like a wonderful idea," Luke's mom said as everyone drifted toward the farm table where the bakery box sat unopened, practically glowing with mystery.

Everyone had tried to guess what the cake might say. The running joke had become a full-on family debate. How could a simple message spelled out in buttercream encompass all they had to celebrate?

"How many letters can a cake hold, anyway?" Travis said, ticking off words on his fingers. "*Adopted, Engaged and Certified.* That seems like a lot of frosting."

"I suggested *Best Day Ever x Three*, but Ella wouldn't let me in on the surprise," Molly said.

"She's been protecting that secret like a dog with a bone," Willow added. Her guide dog, Bear, woofed softly at the word *bone*.

"What if it just says *cake*?" Bethany said, signing the words as she spoke.

Luke ruffled her hair, and everyone laughed.

"Well, there's only one way to find out." Ella grinned as she gestured for Bethany to come forward. Luke placed a gentle hand on her shoulder as they all opened the lid of the cake box together.

Everyone leaned in to take a look, and then a collective *awww* rolled through the room. There, in careful pink frosting script, nestled between vanilla buttercream swirls and tiny paw print decorations were three perfect words.

We're A Family.

Bethany stared at it, eyes wide and shimmering, before turning and hugging Luke around the waist. He bent to hug her, blinking fast. Ella's eyes stung with the quick prick of tears. Even Travis sniffed and claimed the fire-place smoke was getting to him.

"Wait!" Ella cried. She'd almost forgotten. "There's one more reveal."

She dashed to the kitchen and returned with another, smaller bakery box.

"Ta da!" she said. Inside was a round, dog-safe cake—peanut butter and banana flavored, frosted with yogurt and surrounded by crunchy dog biscuits. Two different flavors in accordance with Bethany's wishes. The top-per was shaped like a bone and said *Certified Good Girl.*

Cupcake, Ruby, Snickers and Bear all sniffed the air, noses twitching. Plates and forks appeared, and while Gran sliced the big cake for the humans, Travis divvied up the dog cake among the canine party-goers.

Outside, the snow still fell, quiet and soft. Inside, Ella stood in the middle of it all, marveling at the fact that this was her life now. She looked over at Luke, laughing at something Travis said, but then he caught her gaze and his smile softened.

Yep, this was real. She didn't need to pinch herself to believe it. The cake had already said it best.

"We're a family," Luke whispered into her hair after he'd left Travis chatting with his parents, Molly and Willow.

Ella's brother probably hadn't engaged in this much conversation in months—years, even. Ella hoped he'd find his eagle someday, too, even though he constantly said he was perfectly happy out here in the woods with his dogs.

She wasn't sure she believed him. Not too long ago, a big part of her had doubted she'd ever live this kind of day. She'd spent so much of her life planning other people's futures—training dogs to be helpers, supporting clients through their toughest moments, teaching others to walk by faith and not by sight. But now? Now, it was her turn to be blessed beyond measure. Now, she stood in a room surrounded by the people she loved most. Her mom. Her brother. Her future husband. Her almost-daughter. And their dogs. How could she have nearly let herself miss out on this?

This was her future. This was her life. *This* was love.

And if the past few months had taught Ella anything, it was that love was worth the wait.

* * * * *

Dear Reader,

Welcome to Snowhaven, Alaska, and my brand new Alaskan Hearts series for Love Inspired!

Writing *Training Her Alaskan K-9* felt a lot like coming home. I started my writing career at Love Inspired, and I haven't written for the line in a while, but it's always been in my heart. In a lot of ways, I was like Luke in this book. Writing this story was like finding my way back to a place I'd never really left. Even the name of this series, Alaskan Hearts, is the same as the title of the first book I wrote for Love Inspired back in 2012.

My real-life Cavalier King Charles spaniel Charm became the inspiration for this book when my veterinarian told me she couldn't find Charm's eardrum. Charm was already a registered therapy dog at this point. Once I realized she was indeed deaf, I started to understand that her physical challenges were part of what made her so well-suited to therapy work. God makes the most of our differences every time, and I knew I wanted to write a story celebrating the blessing that Charm has been to so many people, not just in spite of her deafness, but because of it.

I hope you enjoy *Training Her Alaskan K-9*! I love hearing from readers. Feel free to connect with me at teriwilson.net or on Instagram at @teriwilsonauthor. And be sure to look for the second book in the Alaskan Hearts series coming soon.

Grace and blessings,
Teri

Get up to 4 Free Books!

We'll send you 2 free books from each series you try PLUS a free Mystery Gift.

FREE Value Over **$25**

Both the **Love Inspired*** and **Love Inspired*** Suspense series feature compelling novels filled with inspirational romance, faith, forgiveness and hope.

YES! Please send me 2 FREE novels from the Love Inspired or Love Inspired Suspense series and my FREE gift (gift is worth about $10 retail). After receiving them, if I don't wish to receive any more books, I can return the shipping statement marked "cancel." If I don't cancel, I will receive 6 brand-new Love Inspired Larger-Print books or Love Inspired Suspense Larger-Print books every month and be billed just $7.19 each in the U.S. or $7.99 each in Canada. That is a savings of 20% off the cover price. It's quite a bargain! Shipping and handling is just 50¢ per book in the U.S. and $1.25 per book in Canada.* I understand that accepting the 2 free books and gift places me under no obligation to buy anything. I can always return a shipment and cancel at any time by calling the number below. The free books and gift are mine to keep no matter what I decide.

Choose one: ☐ **Love Inspired Larger-Print** (122/322 BPA G36Y) ☐ **Love Inspired Suspense Larger-Print** (107/307 BPA G36Y) ☐ **Or Try Both!** (122/322 & 107/307 BPA G36Z)

Name (please print)

Address   Apt. #

City   State/Province   Zip/Postal Code

Email: Please check this box ☐ if you would like to receive newsletters and promotional emails from Harlequin Enterprises ULC and its affiliates. You can unsubscribe anytime.

> Mail to the **Harlequin Reader Service:**
> **IN U.S.A.:** P.O. Box 1341, Buffalo, NY 14240-8531
> **IN CANADA:** P.O. Box 603, Fort Erie, Ontario L2A 5X3

Want to explore our other series or interested in ebooks? Visit www.ReaderService.com or call 1-800-873-8635.

---

*Terms and prices subject to change without notice. Prices do not include sales taxes, which will be charged (if applicable) based on your state or country of residence. Canadian residents will be charged applicable taxes. Offer not valid in Quebec. This offer is limited to one order per household. Books received may not be as shown. Not valid for current subscribers to the Love Inspired or Love Inspired Suspense series. All orders subject to approval. Credit or debit balances in a customer's account(s) may be offset by any other outstanding balance owed by or to the customer. Please allow 4 to 6 weeks for delivery. Offer available while quantities last.

Your Privacy—Your information is being collected by Harlequin Enterprises ULC, operating as Harlequin Reader Service. For a complete summary of the information we collect, how we use this information and to whom it is disclosed, please visit our privacy notice located at https://corporate. harlequin.com/privacy-notice. Notice to California Residents – Under California law, you have specific rights to control and access your data. For more information on these rights and how to exercise them, visit https://corporate.harlequin.com/california-privacy. For additional information for residents of other U.S. states that provide their residents with certain rights with respect to personal data, visit https://corporate.harlequin.com/other-state-residents-privacy-rights/.

LIRLIS25